the Lacemaker *and the* Princess

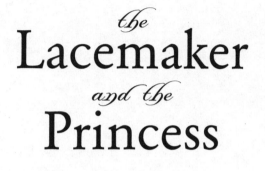

the Lacemaker *and the* Princess

Kimberly Brubaker Bradley

MARGARET K. McELDERRY BOOKS
New York London Toronto Sydney

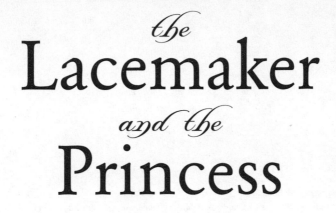

Margaret K. McElderry Books
An imprint of Simon & Schuster Children's Publishing Division
1230 Avenue of the Americas, New York, New York 10020
This book is a work of fiction. Any references to historical events, real people, or real locales are used fictitiously. Other names, characters, places, and incidents are products of the author's imagination, and any resemblance to actual events or locales or persons, living or dead, is entirely coincidental.

Book design by Debra Sfetsios
The text for this book is set in Garamond BE.
Manufactured in the United States of America
10 9 8 7 6 5 4 3
Library of Congress Cataloging-in-Publication Data
Bradley, Kimberly Brubaker.
The lacemaker and the princess / Kimberly Brubaker Bradley.–1st ed.
p. cm.
Summary: In 1788, eleven-year-old Isabelle, living with her lacemaker grandmother and mother near the palace of Versailles, becomes close friends with Marie Antoinette's daughter, Princess Therese, and finds their relationship complicated not only by their different social class but by the growing political unrest and resentment of the French people.
ISBN-13: 978-1-4169-1920-9 (hardcover)
ISBN-10: 1-4169-1920-1 (hardcover)
1. France–History–Louis XVI, 1774–1793–Juvenile fiction. [1. France–History–Louis XVI, 1774–1793–Fiction. 2. Friendship–Fiction. 3. Lace and lace making–Fiction. 4. Princesses–Fiction. 5. Angoulême, Marie-Thérèse Charlotte, duchesse d', 1778–1851–Fiction. 6. France–History–Revolution, 1789–1799–Fiction.] I. Title.
PZ7.B7247Lac 2007
[Fic]–dc22
2006020663

To Karalee Louise Maria Augusta Strieby Harding
(whose best friend calls her Sam)–to Sam,
then, with all my love

April, 1788

Chapter One

When the Princess of Lamballe's lace was ready, Grand-mère decided that I should deliver it. Not because I was responsible–I was not, as she often reminded me. Not because she trusted me–she did not, as I well knew. It was because I was worthless, because Grand-mère had been more than usually unhappy about the lace I'd made the previous day, and because one of the very minor nobles had ordered ten yards of lace–a vast amount–that was to be picked up today, and it wasn't finished. "Stop for George. He'll point you to Her Majesty's rooms," Grand-mère said, stuffing me roughly into my one real dress. "He'll see you don't dawdle, or lose the lace."

George was my older brother. He worked in the stables at the palace of Versailles, caring for the Marquis de Lafayette's carriage horses. Our father had also been a servant of the Marquis. Papa was dead; I never knew him.

"Heaven forbid, lose the lace," murmured Maman, sitting up in her bed in the corner of the room, and crossing herself. Grand-mère was large and fat and mean; Maman was small and crippled and sad. "Take care, Isabelle, will you?" She glanced at Grand-mère. "Perhaps–"

"I don't have a moment to spare, not one moment, not with us so behind," Grand-mère said. She looked at Maman. She did not say it was Maman's fault we were behind with our lacemaking, but she thought it, and Maman and I both knew she was thinking it. Some days Maman's knees and hands hurt so bad that she had to drink laudanum before she could sleep. The medicine made her groggy all the next day, and it made her hands shake, too, which was not good in a lacemaker.

Grand-mère thought that Maman only pretended to be in pain, despite the evidence of her swollen fingers and knees. Grand-mère never believed in any pain she didn't feel herself.

Grand-mère was an evil old goat. She made our house a misery.

Now she poked me with Maman's cane. "Don't you think for a moment that you're off the hook. If it weren't for your shoddy work yesterday, we wouldn't be in such a rush."

This was a lie. The lace I'd ruined yesterday–and I had made a mess of it, the pattern was complicated and I'd gotten confused–was not the lace that was supposed to be ready today. I wasn't trusted to make important lace. But I knew better than to contradict Grand-mère.

"It won't take her long," Maman said. "You, Isabelle, remember you have work waiting when you get home."

I jumped, trying to see myself in the tiny mirror that hung high above the bureau. "Come here," Maman said. She pulled my hair back and powdered it with the hare's foot and powder from the table beside her bed.

"George will be working," I said. He slept at the stables. He was rarely home.

"He can take a moment to help you," Maman said.

Grand-mère grabbed my shoulder and hauled me back to the center of the room. "Hold still." She gathered a handful of lace around the neckline of my dress and quickly sewed it into place. Her needle flashed near my throat. I held still. The lace was not ornate, but all lace was precious. If I moved and Grand-mère stabbed me and I bled on the lace, it would be my fault.

"Some at her wrists, too," suggested Maman.

"She'll ruin it," Grand-mère said. "Foolish girl. She'll fall in a mud puddle or slip on the stairs."

I held my breath. I loved to dress up, and I almost never got to wear the lace we made.

"She'll be careful," said Maman. "Consider that it's the palace, after all. Someone might notice her."

Grand-mère considered. She looked at me the way a hawk might look at a mouse. "Hold up your arms," she commanded at last.

I held them up. "What shall I do?" I said, while Grand-mère whipstitched lace around my sleeves. I tried not to sound excited, in case they changed their minds. "What do I say to the princess?"

I never got to deliver lace, not even when it was only a bourgeoise who'd ordered it, someone who lived and worked right in town. I never got to go to the Château, either, the great palace of Versailles, nor was I allowed to play in the parkland that surrounded it, nor go to the stables and bother my brother, even though he said he didn't mind.

I was a lacemaker, the daughter of a lacemaker, and the granddaughter of one. I had had a needle put into my hands when I was less than five years old. I made lace every day. Also I went to market for our bread and beer, and for the thread and linen that we used. I bought our dinners from the tavern downstairs. I swept out the fires in the mornings, and brought up wood, and emptied chamber pots. I swept our two rooms, and kept them clean. I took our clothes to the laundress down the street. Once we had employed a scullery maid, but that was before Maman's hands got so bad. Now, between the doctor's visits and the laudanum, we needed more money than we had.

I was eleven. Sometimes I still got lost trying to follow a lace pattern, but my stitches were even and my turns were careful and neat. Maman said that sometimes she couldn't tell the difference between my lace and hers. I knew this wasn't true, but I also knew that my lace was not the disgrace Grand-mère said it was. "We Bonnards have to work for our living," Grand-mère had shouted that morning, waving the piece I had ruined beneath my nose. "No one supports us. No one cares to. You, girl, how will you eat if you can't work?" She had flicked a glance at Maman in the bed, and I hated her for it.

Now Grand-mère was shouting again. "You won't speak to the princess! What insolence! As though the governess of the Children of France would bother to speak to such as you! All you are good for is wasting expensive thread," she went on bitterly. "When you get back from the palace, you'll sit on your stool and ply that needle of yours until I'm satisfied."

Grand-mère was never satisfied.

I noticed that she hadn't answered my question, not really, but I didn't want to ask again. She'd start hitting me with the cane if I wasn't careful. Once, she hit me so hard that my shoulder didn't work right for a week.

George would help me. George was my salvation.

Maman produced a ribbon to tie around my neck. Grand-mère shook her head. "Too much."

"Better to have her noticed," Maman said.

Grand-mère scoffed. "Who would notice such a sniveling child?"

"Lacemakers who can't afford fripperies, what kind of message does that send?" Maman murmured. I stole a glance at her, and she smiled. "You look very neat," she told me.

For once Maman won an argument; I left our rooms with a bright silk ribbon around my neck. I clattered down the stairs to the street, and raced down the dusty streets in my little satin shoes, holding tight to the paper-wrapped package of lace. It was a beautiful summer day, all gold sun and blue sky, and I was happy to be set free, if only for a short time. It seemed an age since I'd ventured farther from our apartment than the butcher shop or the chandler.

Versailles's stables, the big stable where the carriage horses lived, and the little stable for riding horses, were immense, but George always cared for the same three teams of horses, and I knew where their stalls were. I found George forking old straw out of one of the stalls into a wheelbarrow. "Maman says you must take me to the palace," I said. "I have lace to deliver." I puffed out my chest a little, pleased with my importance.

"You look beautiful, Bella," George said. He straightened and smiled warmly. "Powdered hair and all."

I twirled around so that he could admire me from all sides, then said, "I must take this to the Princess of Lamballe."

He nodded. "I can walk you to the palace now." He washed his hands in a bucket, then climbed the ladder to the loft where the stable boys slept. When he returned, he was wearing a fresh jacket and his hair had been retied into a queue. He carried his hat under one arm.

"I wish you could powder your hair," I said.

He smiled, but shook his head. "Powder is for postillions," he said. "I'm nothing but a common groom." He put his hat on his head, and took me by the hand. George was fourteen, a head taller than me, and thin as a rail. At first he walked so fast that I had to skip to keep up with him, but then he looked down at me and slowed. "No hurry," he said, and smiled.

"I'll get to meet Her Majesty," I said.

"You won't," he said. "She doesn't speak with lacemakers. Besides, you said it was for the Princess of Lamballe."

"Grand-mère said I should take it to Her Majesty's rooms. Isn't that where the princess lives?"

George laughed at me. "*Her Majesty* is the queen," he said. "The Princess of Lamballe is the queen's great friend. That's why she was named the Dauphin's governess." He paused. "The princess isn't royal. I don't know why they call her princess. She's not a near relation to the king and queen. But she's still very important. She has large rooms all her own."

I knew about the Dauphin, the heir to the throne. The Children of France were the sons and daughter of the king and queen. The oldest of them was Marie Thérèse, nine years old and a disappointment to the nation because she was not a boy. Next came the hope of France, the Dauphin, Louis Joseph, and then the three-year-old Duke of Normandy, Louis Charles. There had been another, a baby named Sophie, but she had died.

The Dauphin's governess would be a very important person, whether she was really a princess or not. "I know Grand-mère said 'Her Majesty's rooms,'" I insisted. I gave a little skip. "To think that someone so important bought our lace!"

George looked down again. "As much lace as the court wears, you'd think they'd keep every lacemaker in France fully occupied." After a pause he added. "Still, you're right. It's a great thing for us if we please her."

If we became fashionable, we would have as many orders for lace as we could fill. We could charge more too. Maman could have all the medicine she needed, and someone besides me could empty the chamber pots. The thought of that was nearly enough for me to love making lace.

The stables fronted the enormous palace. Already we were past the gates of the palisade, fighting our way through the crowd. The courtyard was like a marketplace, full of peasants and merchants and beggars. One fashionable man rushed by on very high heels, the skirts of his long yellow coat flapping. He held his wig to his head with one hand. I stared. The coat was silk, I was sure. I'd felt a piece of silk once, so smooth under the fingers, and light, and rich.

"Listen," said George. He stopped and lifted my chin. "You see why this is important, don't you?" I nodded, but he continued to look straight into my eyes. "This is the first time an important person ever ordered Maman's lace. You won't see the princess, but be sure you act respectful to everybody you do meet."

"Grand-mère made the lace," I said. "Not Maman."

"That's not my point," George said.

I frowned. "I know how to behave."

He patted my chin. "I know you do, *ma belle*. Just be sure that you actually behave as well as you know how."

"*Ma belle*" meant "my beautiful one." It was a play on my

name, Isabelle. Only George ever called me beautiful.

I saw the enormous palace of Versailles from the town every day. It was like a mountain, part of the scenery; I hardly noticed it. But now, as we made our way closer, it seemed to grow bigger and bigger, more and more ornate. "This is nothing," George replied, when I said so. "You should see the back side, and the gardens."

We stopped at a booth near a door to the inside, where a man had a collection of small swords. George handed the man a few coins; he bowed, and handed George a sword. George buckled it around his waist.

"I'm renting it," he explained. "Men must wear a hat and a sword to enter Versailles."

"You aren't a man," I said.

George frowned. "I am too. The Marquis de Lafayette was hardly older than me when he joined the army."

"You're not a marquis."

He pushed me through the door. "Up that stairway over there. That's the Queen's Stairway." He pushed harder. "Move, Isabelle."

I was too busy staring. The palace was as grand as I'd always imagined. The stairs were marble, and so were the banisters, and the rail. The floors were marble tiles and the ceilings were hung with carvings painted gold. Every corner held a statue; every open spot a piece of furniture so beautifully carved and painted I wondered that anyone dared sit upon it.

Yet there was a beggar sitting on a tapestry-covered bench–a one-eyed beggar wearing a hat and sword. "Look!" I whispered.

"Hush!" said George.

The smell was awful; it grew worse as we picked our way up

the stairs. It smelled like the latrine in the back of our courtyard at home, only stronger. I lifted my sleeve and buried my nose in my lace cuff.

A beautiful woman swept down the stairs in wide panniered skirts and a tall, tall wig. The crowd made way for her, pressing George and me close against the rail. The woman looked neither right nor left; she expected everyone to give her room. *Her Majesty,* I thought. I elbowed George. "Is that–"

"It's a nobody," he said. "Some country courtier begging a favor. Come on."

"How do you know?"

"I know. When you see them often enough, you can tell the difference, the ones who are important and the ones who aren't."

At the top of the stairs was an enormous guardroom, black and red marble, the ceiling painted with pictures of cherubs and people wearing sheets. A huge fire blazed on golden andirons, and over it three guards in uniform were cooking sausages. One of them looked barely older than George. More guards played cards at a small table near the door, and a little black dog lay at their feet.

The crowd had thinned near the doorway of the room. George put the lace parcel into my hands and gave me another push, so that I fell a few steps across the threshold. "Go ahead," he whispered. "When you're done, go out just the way you came in."

"Wait," I said, "what do I–" It was no use. He had already turned and ducked back into the crowd.

I shouldered my way past the last few people and took one step into the cavernous room. The walls towered over me. One of the card-playing guards stood and came toward me. He was not one of the young ones; he was broad-shouldered, bearded, and tall. "Your purpose, little miss?"

I curtsied. "Please, sir, I come to bring lace ordered by the Princess of Lamballe."

The first guard spoke to another, who went out a small door in the back of the room. He came back with a girl not much older than myself. She was dressed in a black gown, possibly silk, I thought, but without panniers or lace; even I could see she was a servant of some sort.

"Give it to Jeannette, here," said the first guard. "She'll see the princess gets it."

I didn't think Maman would like me handing our lace to a servant named Jeannette. Plus I still hoped to catch a glimpse of someone important. "But sir," I said, clutching the package more tightly. "That's not the princess. And the payment–" I didn't know, actually, if I was supposed to collect any money. Grand-mère hadn't said. I didn't know how much she wanted for the lace.

Jeannette marched forward. "You'll have to send a bill, then, won't you?" she said. She snatched the parcel out of my hands. "The nerve of these tradespeople!" She laughed, and the guards joined in.

"But how will I know the princess–"

The big guard cut me off. He shepherded me out of the room. "Don't worry, little bourgeoise," he said. "Jeannette will see that the lace comes to no harm."

He was mocking me, laughing at my concern. My face flamed with anger. I wanted to kick him, hard, and run after that Jeannette. I wanted to tell him how Maman and Grand-mère had worked over that lace, how many hours it had taken them to make it, how many hours I myself worked every day. I opened my mouth to say something. The guard covered my mouth with his hand. He picked me up and carried me to the door. My skirts hampered my kicking, but I still landed several good blows. "OUT," he roared, setting me down in the hallway and shoving me toward the stairs.

Perhaps I had not been respectful, as George had said, but no one in the hallway seemed to notice. I stood in the midst of a dozen people, maybe more. I didn't see any beggars now; everyone was richly dressed, gorgeously dressed, dazzling embroidery and more lace than I'd ever imagined. They were all hurrying one direction or another as fast as they could. The instant my guard got rid of me, a man stepped in front of him, and began talking very fast. He said he had business with Her Majesty.

"Her Majesty is not in," the guard informed him. The man slunk away.

The red marble walls looked like giant slabs of beef with white veins of fat running through them. The odor of the guards' sausages filled the air, masking the smells of the puddles fermenting on the staircase. I didn't see George anywhere.

Rotten boy, gone back to the stables already, I thought. And was that all I was supposed to have done with the lace? It didn't seem worth the trouble of dressing up. Perhaps I should have demanded payment. Perhaps I had failed. Maman would say so, and sigh. Grand-mère would make me sit on my chair for hours. I'd be plying my needle by candlelight today.

My stomach rumbled. What I wouldn't give for a sausage!

A finely dressed lady bumped into me. She gave off an odor of perfume almost as offensive as the general stench. "Watch what you're about, little girl!" she said. I curtsied and apologized, but she didn't notice. She'd already hurried by. I was not important enough to pay attention to.

I've been abandoned, I thought. *Abandoned and ignored, inside the Palace of Versailles.* My heart gave a skip. What a wonderful place to be ignored! I thought one last time of Grand-mère and her stool. Then, instead of heading down the queen's staircase toward home, I turned right and started down a long, long hall. I may have failed in my errand, but no one would know it until I went home.

Chapter Two

Enormous hallways; dozens upon dozens of rooms. The splendor went on forever, with each new scene as grand as the last. After a while my eyes grew numb to it; I no longer saw the paintings, carvings, and tapestries as anything but swirls of color. My stomach grumbled. I found a staircase–much smaller this time–and went down to the ground floor, and then to the basement. The odor of cooking grew stronger. I followed my nose around the winding corridors, sniffing like a rabbit, until I came to a vast room with more fireplaces and spits than I would have thought possible.

"Quick!" I said to a small boy standing near the door. "Sausages! Hurry!" He jumped up, alarmed, and rushed to put hot sausages into a dish. "And some bread," I said. He laid a bun across the sausages and thrust the whole into my hands. I turned and ran out without thanking him. Already I had learned from Jeannette, and from the people in the halls–the higher servants bossed anyone beneath them. The lesser nobility bossed the servants. I was sure the higher nobility must boss the lesser, and so forth right up to the king. No one could boss him; only God. Because I bossed the kitchen boy, he naturally assumed I outranked him. If I pretended to be important, I could have my way.

The sausages were delicious. Grease ran down my chin, but I mopped it up with a crust of the bread and didn't drip onto my dress. I went back to the first floor and kept exploring.

The windowless hallways were lit with sconces holding several candles apiece. I marveled at them. At home we sometimes lit a single candle, in winter when we needed light to make lace by. After a while I noticed a boy carrying a stool and a basket down the hall in front of me. At each sconce he would climb onto the stool, remove the nearly spent candles, and replace them with long fresh ones from his basket. I watched him. *Boring work,* I thought, but not nearly as boring as making lace. "What do you do with the candle stubs?" I asked.

He looked down. "The nobles that have the rights of the candles sell them, of course."

"Which nobles?"

"Whichever ones have the rights of those candles. The king gives them the rights." He climbed down from the stool. "Do you need some?"

"No." Though if they were at a good price, Maman might be interested.

He made a face. "What do you care, then, what I do?"

I followed him to the next sconce. "Do you change candles all day?"

"As does my father," said the boy. "As did his father before him, rest his soul."

That was the way it always worked. I made lace because my mother did. George cared for horses like our father had. The Dauphin would be the next king. Birth was everything. "Do you like it?" I asked.

"Why do you care? Nosy girl. Who are you? Somebody's servant?"

His tone was curious, not insolent. "I'm Isabelle Bonnard," I said. "I make lace–as does my mother, as did her mother, rest her soul." Grand-mère was Papa's mother, not Maman's.

The candle boy grinned at me. "I'm Pierre," he said.

Before he could say more, there was a bustle at the end of the hallway. The gentlemen and ladies moving through the hall all surged in that direction. I couldn't see anything, but Pierre, on his stool, could. "Her Majesty," he said. "She has finished her dinner."

"Oh! Can I see her?"

"Hurry," he said, "before the crowd gets too thick."

I rushed forward. My chance to see the queen! More and more people jammed the corridor; everyone wanted the queen. Their voices filled the air, asking favors, paying compliments.

One man pushed me sideways. I stumbled, and fell against another man. He pushed me away from him, back onto the first man, and I fell against his chest. "Stupid girl–" He shoved me, harder this time, back against the second man, who gave an angry snort and pushed me hard. I lost my feet entirely and began to panic. I would be trampled; I would be killed. A man's heel stabbed my calf. A woman's fan caught the edge of my lace cuff, and snapped. "Idiot!" The woman pummeled me.

"George!" I screamed. I knew it was useless, but George had always saved me. Now I fell against a guard, who hooked his elbow under mine and sent me flying. I sprawled across a sudden opening in the crowd, right at the foot of another lady, and suddenly everything went still. I sat up, dazed. Someone had knocked me in the mouth, and I could taste blood.

"Oh, the poor thing!" The lady bent over me. "Little one, are you all right? How frightened you must be! Oh, she's bleeding–a handkerchief, quick!"

In the stillness a dozen people thrust out handkerchiefs–lace-trimmed silk and linen, very fine. The lady grabbed the closest and held it to my mouth. "Does it hurt?" she asked, helping me to my feet.

"No, ma'am," I said. I tried to take the handkerchief away–I should not bleed on something so expensive–but the lady shook her head at me and pressed the handkerchief more firmly.

She wore a plain white gown and her hair was tied back loosely under her cap. She did not wear jewels or powder. But she carried herself with a hauteur that was unmistakable. I knew, too, that no one else could have so completely silenced the crowd. She smiled at me kindly, and with her free hand brushed my tousled hair back from my face. "Your Majesty," I said, and curtsied to the queen.

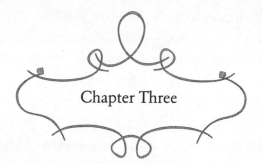

Chapter Three

It wasn't much of a curtsy since she was still holding the handkerchief to my face. The queen laughed, a lovely tinkling sound. The crowd kept their distance a few feet away. Their voices starting up again sounded like the hum of faraway bees. The queen did not regard them; it was as though they did not exist, as though she and I were the only two people in the world. "You are so beautiful!" she said. "Who are you? Where are you from? Why are you at Versailles?"

"I am called Isabelle Bonnard," I said. "My family are lacemakers in town. I came to deliver lace for the Princess of Lamballe."

"For the princess!" she said, laughing a little. "But why not for me?"

She was so lovely and graceful. She put the grand palace to shame. "The Princess of Lamballe bought our lace," I said. "You could have it for free."

Her smile deepened. She slipped her hand in mine. "Have you already been taught to curry royal favor?"

I looked away. I had been taught to curry favor from the very minor nobles; starting today, I had hoped to please the Princess of Lamballe. Even in my wildest dreams I had not imagined so much as speaking to the queen. "I should scarce hope to do so," I murmured. "But if I did please Your Majesty, I should be very glad."

"What would you gain, a child like you?"

"It would pay you back," I said. "For saving me."

She put her arm around my shoulder and drew me closer to her. "Were you so frightened, then?"

I nodded. "I thought I would be trampled. No one cared whether they hurt me."

The queen dropped her voice to a whisper. "These halls are no place for children. My daughter also dislikes the crowds. Would you like to meet her? She would like that, I think; she's lonely today, dear Ernestine is away."

"If it please Your Majesty," I said, "I should be honored. I've never met a princess before."

The queen frowned. "You must not think of her as a princess. Mousseline is only a child. I refuse to allow her position to burden her. She plays with her playmates in an ordinary way, like any other child."

I didn't have playmates to play with. I knew a few girls who lived on the same street as me, but all of us had work to do.

The queen and I set off down the corridor. She held my hand. The courtiers began to shout at her again, but she ignored them entirely and asked me questions instead. Where did I live? On the main street of the town, above a tavern. How old was I? Eleven.

"You look younger," the queen said. "Mousseline is only nine, but she is every bit as tall as you." "Mousseline" meant "muslin," a delicate cloth. I wished my mother had a tender nickname for me.

As we walked, the swarm of courtiers kept pace with us. The

queen continued to ignore them, so I did too. It grew more difficult as we progressed. Shouts of "Your Majesty! Your Majesty!" filled my ears until I could barely answer the queen. We went into a room, and through it to another, leaving most of the crowd behind. A servant shut a door, and the noise dropped. A crease on the queen's forehead eased. I hadn't noticed it until it disappeared. "So many people," she murmured, passing her hand briefly over her eyes. "These are my daughter's rooms. Come, we will find her."

The rooms all connected with one another. When we entered the third, the women inside it stood up at once, and curtsied low. A little girl sitting among them stood up too. She set down the embroidery frame she was holding and dutifully curtsied, but not as far down as the women had. The queen went forward and embraced her. The girl hugged her back, but did not smile. Her face was sullen and brooding.

"Still unhappy?" the queen asked, lifting her chin.

"Ernestine is not here," the girl said, in an unpleasant whine. "Madame de Polignac does not please me, and my thread is all in knots."

The queen laughed her tiny tinkling laugh, and the girl stiffened. If the queen noticed, she gave no sign. "I have found you a friend for today," she said, stroking her daughter's head, "so you need not be so sad over Ernestine."

"I'm not sad over Ernestine," said the princess. "I'm bored and I'm cross and I'm tired." She looked at me. "What do we call her?"

I made my best curtsy. "Isabelle Bonnard, mademoiselle."

"Yes," she said impatiently, "but what do we *call* her?"

To my surprise the queen turned and looked at me thoughtfully.

"Oh, I think Isabelle is a fine name for her," she said. "She's pretty, and it's a nice name."

"I don't like it," said the princess.

"It suits her," said the queen.

This made no sense to me, but I didn't say anything. "Very well," the princess said. She turned to me, still without smiling. "I won't do my embroidery, then. We will walk outside together, and I will show you my sheep."

Somehow I found being ordered around by one of the Children of France much more pleasant than being ordered around by Grand-mère. I curtsied again. "Yes, Your Highness," I said. Was that right? I knew to always say "Your Majesty" to the queen.

The queen laughed. "No, no," she said. "You must call her Thérèse. You are playmates. She won't have any fun if she is always being made to feel like a princess."

Thérèse pursed her lips. She looked as though she preferred to feel like a princess. I didn't blame her. If I were a princess, I'd make people curtsy to me all the time. Curtsy, and kiss my hands.

Thérèse said good-bye to her mother and walked out one of the tall side doors. She beckoned impatiently, and I followed, in a daze. The queen of France wishing that I should play with her daughter? As well the heavens should open up, and my dead father fly down to embrace me. But when I stubbed my toe on the pebbled path, the pain was real. I was not dreaming.

A woman dressed in somber gray trailed after us. "Is that your governess?" I whispered. She was not nearly as grand as I'd imagined the Princess of Lamballe to be. The little princess ignored me. I hurried after her. Gathering my courage, I said, "Thérèse!"

She spun around, and for a moment I thought she was angry

that I'd used her name. But she looked at me calmly, almost unemotionally.

"Is that your governess?" I repeated. "Is she the Princess of Lamballe?"

Thérèse glanced back. "No. The princess isn't my governess; Madame de Polignac is. The princess is my brother's governess. And that woman is only one of the undergovernesses. We can ignore her. She'll follow us all around, but she won't get in our way."

We went quickly down some stone steps and out onto a wide path flanked by trees. Here and there a statue on a pedestal rose high above us. Thérèse saw me glance at one. "Zeus," she said.

The statue was a man with a cloth draped around his middle. He looked strong and angry. I nodded. "Was he a king?"

Thérèse gave a snort of laughter. "He's from Greek mythology," she said. "Don't you know that?"

I had never heard of Greek mythology. "No," I said. I stopped on the path. I felt a bit annoyed. I did not mind being told what to do by this grim little princess, but I did not like her laughing at me.

Thérèse stopped too, her hands on her hips. She did not look angry; she was still laughing a little, and she looked more agreeable than when we'd first met. "Have you never studied mythology?" I shook my head.

"Never at all?"

"No."

"Do you know Latin?"

"No."

"Geography."

"No." I could feel my temper rising.

"The use of the globes?"

"No."

Thérèse laughed again. "Do you know *anything*?" she asked.

I took a deep breath. "I know how to make needle lace and sew and hem and build a fire and tend it and clean the ashes out. I can make tea and toast and cook a chicken if I have to. I can empty chamber pots and scrub floors and beat the dust from rugs. I know how to do all of that, and do it well."

Thérèse's eyes had widened as I spoke. "Oh," she said, "how *awful*."

Her sincerity surprised me so much that my budding anger vanished. "Well, yes," I said. "It is."

"You don't mind being here with me, then," she said.

"No," I said. "I like it."

"Good," she said. "I thought maybe it was something they were making you do."

I didn't understand that, but I let it pass. "Come," she said. We began walking again. Several yards behind us the gray-gowned servant began walking again too. I had not noticed, but she must have stopped when Thérèse did.

The path was lined with carefully spaced young trees. The breeze blew through them, and in their dappled shade the summer's heat was not unpleasant. I thought of how stuffy our room at home grew each afternoon. How lucky I was, to be walking with Thérèse! I looked her over as we walked. Her dress was not any fancier than my own, except that it had wider panniers and the cloth itself was finer. Her hair was not powdered, and she did not have a ribbon around her neck. She did not look in any way like a king's child. Her face was thin, her gray eyes sad.

I was panting a little, from the fast pace Thérèse set. "Who is Ernestine?" I asked.

"She's just Ernestine," said Thérèse. "She comes in the morning and stays with me all day. She goes home at night. But today a boy came to say she couldn't come."

"Was she sick?"

"I don't know."

"Was it the candle boy who came to tell you? The one named Pierre?"

Thérèse raised her eyebrows. "How should I know?" After a pause she added, "There are hundreds of candle changers. Some of them are men. I don't know their names."

"There can't be *hundreds,*" I said.

Her eyebrows went up; she looked miffed again. "Hundreds," she repeated firmly. She paused, then asked, "*What* was your name again?"

"Isabelle. Isabelle Bonnard."

"Isabelle," repeated Thérèse, "and we are to call you Isabelle."

"What else would you call me?" I said.

"Oh," said Thérèse, "Ernestine's name isn't really Ernestine. And Isabelle." She wrinkled her nose. "It's not a *fashionable* name, is it?"

I had never thought of whether my name was fashionable or not. "What difference does that make?"

Thérèse shrugged. "My mother likes everything to be fashionable," she said. "The French court is the most fashionable court in the world."

As we walked, she began to tell me about her flock of sheep, which she visited every day. "Do you take care of them?" I asked. It was difficult to imagine, but then, so was everything else about the palace.

"Sometimes I feed them," she said. "If I'm very quiet, they will eat from my hand. But if I'm not quiet, they run, and leap!" Her quiet face became animated. "Sheep are funny," she said.

I had never thought of sheep as anything but something to eat. We had mutton often. I said so.

"Yes," Thérèse agreed, "and leg of lamb in the springtime is very good. But not these sheep. These sheep are–" Suddenly she jumped. Her face froze. "Do not pay any attention to them," she whispered.

"To whom?" I looked through the grove of trees, and saw a pair of boys running toward us. Unlike Thérèse, they were gorgeously dressed, all over velvet and embroidery and gold lace. They were older than she was by a couple of years, and brawny. Their faces looked pleasant enough until they saw us, and then their grins took on a malevolent air.

"What ho!" cried the older boy. "Madame Royale! And one of her little beggar friends."

Thérèse's whole body stiffened. She continued to walk straight forward. I stepped into place close beside her without a word.

"Have to play with servants, don't you?" continued the older boy. "Your mama's hired you some friends."

Thérèse said nothing. I glanced over my shoulder at the undergoverness. Her face was nearly as impassive as Thérèse's.

"Where's your brother?" the younger boy asked. "How come he's not here? Where's the Dauphin, eh?"

"Oh, look, he's not outside," the older one said, looking about him with an expression of mock surprise. "Why doesn't he play with you in the sunshine? He must be–"

"My brother the Dauphin is with his tutor," Thérèse said evenly, with an edge in her voice that could have cut steel. "He has many things to learn for the day when he becomes the king of France."

"Ah, yes, learning," the younger boy said. "No doubt the king of France must be very learned."

I didn't understand the sarcasm in his voice. I didn't understand who these boys were, or why they thought they were allowed to speak to Thérèse this way.

"You forget yourself," I said, staring the younger one in the eye. He was not any bigger than me. "Certainly no gentleman would speak so to one of the Children of France."

"Ooh!" he said. "The servant girl speaks!"

"We don't have to be gentlemen," the older one said. "Don't kid yourself, little puss." He chucked me under the chin the way you would a baby. Without thinking, I whirled around and went to kick him in the shin. For the second time that day my skirts got in my way. Instead of kicking the boy, I tripped him. He fell back hard onto the dirt path. His eyes flared up with anger.

"Oh, I beg your pardon," I said, as sweetly sarcastic as I could manage. "I do hope I haven't hurt you."

The younger boy was howling with laughter. "She got you!" he said. "You didn't even see that coming!"

The older one flushed red. He got up, gave Thérèse and me a furious look, and began to stalk back to the palace. The back of his velvet breeches were covered in mud. "I'm telling my papa!" he yelled.

"Go ahead!" Thérèse yelled back. "Whining baby!"

I was beginning to feel panicked. Whoever that boy was, if he complained that I had ruined his clothing–I knew what cloth cost, a fine velvet court suit like that would cost more than

George made in half a year. We could never pay for it.

"That fixed them," Thérèse said with satisfaction. "He hates having his clothes dirtied. He'll stay away from *you*."

"Oh, no," I moaned. "I'll be in horrible trouble. Who was he? Someone important?"

Thérèse stared in delighted amazement. "Important? You didn't know?" She laughed aloud. "Those were my cousins. The younger one is the Duke of Berry, and that horrid great lout is the Duke of Angoulême."

I could feel the blood draining down from my face. The sons of the Count of Artois, the king's youngest brother! My family would be ruined, for my temper and my folly. What had George said? Behave the way I knew to, not the way I usually did.

Thérèse grabbed my arm. "Don't look like that," she said. "They won't tell anybody. They won't dare, because if they did, I'd tell the king my father what they said about Joseph."

"Joseph?"

"My brother," she said impatiently. "The Dauphin."

"Why did they say it? Where is the Dauphin?"

Thérèse's face resumed its shuttered look. "He is with his tutor," she said.

We stayed in the park for several hours, watching the sheep and then wandering past the statues and ponds. The fountains were all turned off, the water motionless in the basins. "It costs too much to run them all the time," Thérèse said. "They only run when my father the king is nearby."

We were in sight of the palace again. George was right, the back side was even more beautiful and impressive than the front. The riches of the king and queen were beyond belief. I knew Thérèse was lying about the fountains.

At the door of the palace she paused. I paused too, not sure what she wanted me to do. "Ernestine usually goes home now," she said at last.

"Oh," I said. "Do you want me to leave?" The sun was low in the sky. Grand-mère would be furious; Maman would be worried.

"Yes," Thérèse said. She frowned. "Will you come back?"

"Do you want me to?"

Her eyes looked sad again, almost haunted. "If you want to," she said. "I could command you to–but I'd rather not–my cousins called you a servant–"

"I'm not a servant," I said. "I'm a lacemaker, a tradesperson, a bourgeoise."

Thérèse hesitated. "I would rather you were only a girl."

I didn't know what to say. "I liked your sheep," I said at last. "I liked walking with you."

For one brief moment her eyes lit. Then one of the servants opened the door in front of us. Thérèse nodded to her and glided over the threshold. "Come tomorrow," she said, looking back at me. "Come as soon as you can. I'll show you the Hamlet, my mother's farm."

She shut the door and I began the long walk around the wings of the palace. I had George to love me, but he worked all the time. I never realized how lonely I was until I saw that Thérèse was that lonely too.

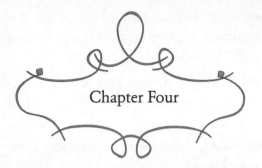

Chapter Four

I would be whipped for my lateness, of course. The low sun cast long shadows by the time I reached the town streets. All the shopkeepers had put up their awnings and closed their storefronts. I was later even than I'd feared. I began to run. My slippers weren't sturdy enough for all the walking I'd done that day, and one of them slipped off my heel. I stumbled, hit the edge of the stone curb, and fell. Horses had been by recently. My sleeve, with its beautiful lace, squished into a steaming green pile of fresh manure.

Ruined. It had taken Maman a day to make it.

I picked myself up, but now I didn't dare go home. My stomach ached–Thérèse had not offered me anything to eat, and the sausages I'd scammed from the kitchen boy were no more than a memory–and as soon as Grand-mère saw my dress, I would be beaten as I had never been beaten before. I would be sent to bed hungry.

I would rather be later still than hungry all night. I turned and went back to the stables. George was sitting on an overturned bucket near his horses' stalls, whittling a scrap of wood. He whistled when he saw me. "Grand-mère kick you out?"

"I didn't go home," I said.

"I don't blame you. Hungry?" He pulled half a loaf of bread out of the pocket of his work frock and tossed it to me. "There's water over there. You might wash."

"It won't make any difference," I said.

"You'd smell better," he said. I shrugged. "As you like," he said. "It's a smell I'm used to."

We sat in silence. All around us horses chewed their hay. There were over three hundred horses in the big stable, to say nothing of the riding horses next door. After a while George said, "I'm sorry, Bella. But you know you can't spend the night here."

I nodded. The stars were coming out now, one by one in the darkening sky. I was as tired as I'd ever been. If I shut my eyes, I could see Her Majesty, smiling at me.

"She's like an angel," I said.

"Who?"

"Her Majesty."

George straightened up. "You got a glimpse of her, then? The queen?"

"She took me to see Madame Royale," I said. "Thérèse. We spent the whole afternoon in the gardens."

George laughed. "You're lying!"

"No–"

"You spent the day with Madame Royale?"

"Thérèse. She's odd, you know, but I like her." I was so tired I hardly knew what I was saying.

"You are not lying?"

I couldn't make up such an incredible lie. "Of course not," I said.

"You swear on our father's grave–"

"If I knew where it was, I would swear on it." Our father had gone with the marquis to America, to fight the British. He'd died of dysentery in a place called Virginia.

George laughed. "If that's really true, you don't need to fear going home. Grand-mère will forgive you anything, if you've really made friends with the daughter of Marie Antoinette."

George was right. On his instructions, I bounced through the door of our apartment, singing, "I spent the day with Madame Royale!" Grand-mère's look of vivid fury vanished in an instant.

Still she grabbed Maman's cane, and whacked me once across the backside. "You're not lying? If you're lying, stupid girl–"

I was not lying, and a few quick answers to her questions satisfied her of the truth. Grand-mère nearly danced with glee.

"Oh, wonderful–a happy day–a joyous day, the Virgin be praised–get that dress off–a bath, you must have a bath–glory to the saints–are you hungry, my dear?"

"Could you not have sent word?" Maman said. "I was afraid you'd come to harm."

I looked at her anxious face. "No, Maman," I said. "I don't see how I could have."

This was a half-truth at best. I knew I could have gone straight home instead of running about the palace for hours.

"Would she not have let you send a servant?" Maman persisted.

"I'm sorry, Maman," I said. "I didn't think of it." I threw my arms around her and hugged her hard, then regretted it when she flinched. "Is the pain very bad today?" I whispered.

"Nothing to speak of," she whispered back. Yet there was a glass of laudanum next to her bed.

Grand-mère stripped my dress off as if I were a tiny child. Maman helped me out of my shift, and Grand-mère poured hot water from the kettle and cold water from the bucket into our rarely used hip bath.

"She won't be hungry. They'll have fed her at the palace, of course." That was Grand-mère.

"I am hungry. We didn't take time to eat." The warm water felt blissful on my aching feet. Maman rubbed soap into a cloth and washed my face, my arms.

"What was she like?" Maman asked.

"Beautiful. More beautiful than I ever dreamed."

"Huh," said Grand-mère. "I've never heard the little chit called a beauty."

"Not Thérèse," I said, "the queen."

Grand-mère reached forward to pinch me. "Rude girl! Have you no manners? You don't call Madame Royale by her Christian name!"

"Yes, I do," I said. "They said to." Maman poured the water through my hair. Her hand on my back was gentle, as gentle as I ever remembered. A perfect end to my perfect day.

Grand-mère grunted. Maman smiled. "Very well," she said. "Very well done, Isabelle."

I shut my eyes. The tiniest edge of worry crept into my bliss. Thérèse wanted me to be her friend–someone she didn't have to pay. But that was not what Maman and Grand-mère expected at all.

The next morning Grand-mère bundled me out of bed before the sun had fairly risen. She and Maman had cleaned my dress in the night, sponging the sleeve until it was spotless and replacing the ruined lace with fresh. While I ate my bread and drank my bowl of milk, Grand-mère brushed my hair and pinned it up. "How does the little princess wear her hair?" she asked.

"Down," I said. I hated wearing my hair up. "Plain and unpowdered."

Grand-mère grunted. She took my hair back down. "Ribbons?"

"Yes," I said. "Lots and lots of ribbons."

If I said Thérèse ate beefsteak for breakfast, would Grand-mère fetch me some from the butcher's? It was almost worth trying. She threaded ribbons through my curls. Maman thrust a parcel into my hands. "A small gift," she said, "to Her Majesty the queen, for her very great kindness to you."

"Now look," Grand-mère said. She grabbed my arm so hard I thought she'd bruise me, and marched me down the stairs to the street. "You stay at that palace as long as they allow it. You go along with anything that girl wants you to do. Please her, you hear?" She licked the space where her front teeth used to be and rubbed her hands together. "If we find favor with Her Majesty, we could be rich."

Grand-mère was a nasty old goat, but I delighted in being sent back to the palace. I ran through the streets, holding my skirts high. This time I didn't look for the queen in her rooms. I ran straight through the ground floor, around the back, and presented myself at the same door where Thérèse had left me the night before. A maidservant answered my knock. "I'm here for–"

Before I could finish, someone inside called out "Clochette!" in a glad voice. Thérèse ran toward me happily. "Clochette!" she said again. "I'm so glad you've come back. Meet Ernestine."

"Isabelle," I corrected her. "I brought you a gift–" But my hands were empty–somehow, I'd dropped the parcel. "I meant to bring–"

Thérèse dragged me to a sofa where a small dark-haired girl sat. "Ernestine, meet Clochette," Thérèse said. "Maman found her for me yesterday, when you were gone. *Clochette,* this is Ernestine."

"Hello," I said.

Ernestine smiled in a friendly way. "Hello," she said. "You're Clochette?"

"I am not," I said. "I'm Isabelle. Isabelle Bonnard." I wrinkled my brow at Thérèse. "You're to call me Isabelle, remember? The queen your mother said so."

Thérèse's eyes danced. "I remember," she said, "but I'd rather call you Clochette. I was up half the night wondering if you'd come back, and I thought, I should like to call her Clochette." She grabbed my arm. "Please," she wheedled. "It's such a *fashionable* name."

"I'm not a fashionable person," I said. "I like my own name."

"And you shall have it," Thérèse said, sounding very much like a princess. "Everywhere but here. Because we are going to be best friends, and sometimes best friends have little pet names for each other, you know."

"My brother calls me Bella," I said.

Thérèse smiled. "And I call you Clochette." She leaned over and kissed my cheek.

"All right," I said. "As Your Highness pleases."

"No!" said Thérèse. "Not 'as Your Highness.' As your very great friend Thérèse pleases."

"As my very great friend Thérèse pleases," I repeated. "She, and she alone, may call me Clochette." Then I looked at Ernestine and added, "And Ernestine too, if she wants to."

Thérèse turned to Ernestine. "I told you you would like her!" she said.

I felt a glow in my insides that warmed my whole soul. I didn't care what Grand-mère wanted. Thérèse and I would be friends.

Chapter Five

Ernestine was smaller than Thérèse, and dark haired, with small features and bright dark eyes. Her eyes and her whole face smiled at me. She and Thérèse were dressed identically; aside from their coloring, they looked very much alike. "Were you sick yesterday?" I asked her.

A frown passed like a shadow over her face. "My mother was," she said. "She's a bit better today."

Thérèse pulled her off the sofa. "Ernestine is sad when her mother is sick," she said. "We won't think about it." Ernestine shook her head slightly. "I said we're not to think about it," Thérèse repeated. "You must not, Ernestine."

Ernestine sighed. "No. I must not."

"No sad things today," Thérèse went on. "And no lessons, either, not today. We'll go out to the gardens. Ernestine and I have our own beds, Clochette. We will tell the gardeners to turn over one for you, too. Oh!" She turned to one of the maidservants. "Send Madame Seamstress in, quick!"

The girl turned and rushed out. "You have to be dressed like us," Thérèse said.

My dress was pretty and had more ribbons than theirs. My lace was very nice. I said so.

"Yes," said Thérèse impatiently. "You look fine, I don't care what you wear, but Maman won't like it if we aren't dressed exactly the same."

"Otherwise, Thérèse might think herself above us," said Ernestine, a grin returning to her face. "She might think she's a princess or something, if her dresses were finer than ours."

"But she is a princess," I said.

"Yes. It's silly," said Thérèse. "Still, I suppose you won't mind it, will you? Only, your court dresses will have to stay here. You'll have to put your regular clothes back on when you go home."

Madame Seamstress measured my height and waist and arms with string, and then Ernestine, Thérèse, and I ran outside. We spent the morning working in their gardens, which were big squares of earth filled with flowers and vegetable plants. They had to show me what to pull and what to leave planted; I'd never seen vegetables growing in the earth. They looked shocked when I said so. "No one farms in town," I explained. "The vegetables are brought in from the country. We buy them at the market."

Thérèse sniffed. "How ignorant you are."

"I know how to–"

She waved her hand. "Yes, yes, you know many important things," she said. "However, you don't know many things that practically everyone else knows. I think you've lived a very sheltered life."

I started to argue, but bit back my retort. What good would it do? Instead I applied myself to learning the difference between a sweet pea and a weed, a ripe green bean and an immature one.

Ernestine came to my side. "Have you really never seen fields?" she asked. "Never seen people working in them? Have you never managed to leave town at all?"

I liked the way she said "managed." She at least seemed to understand more of what my life was like. I wondered where Ernestine came from. Probably her parents were minor nobles; if she had a title, certainly Thérèse would have said so. "Almost never," I said. "George took me up on a wagon once, for a ride. We could see workers far away, but we never drove close."

"Sometimes the food we eat comes from our very own garden," Thérèse said proudly. "We grow it ourselves."

I had seen great wagonloads of vegetables trundle through town, destined for the kitchens at Versailles. I wondered how much food really came from Thérèse's little plot.

Far off across the parkland we could see a hunting party, all on horseback galloping together. Thérèse shielded her eyes and looked at them longingly. "The king my father is riding his new bay horse today," she said. "See there?"

I could see a large man on a bay horse in the front of the group. Everyone I knew said the king was a lumpish oaf–kingly, of course, but not handsome like his grandfather, the old king, had been. From this far away, however, he looked as graceful as his companions.

"Can you ride a horse?" Thérèse asked me.

"I don't know," I said. "I suppose I could. It doesn't look difficult."

"Have you ever done it?" she shot back.

"No," I said, "but I've been around horses. My brother works in the stables."

Both girls stared.

"It's a fine job," I said, a little defensively. "He works for the Marquis de Lafayette."

"You're lucky, having a brother," Ernestine said. "My father would give anything for a son."

"Do you have a father?" I asked.

"Yes."

"Then we're even," I said. "Mine's dead. He went with the Marquis to America, years ago, and died there."

Thérèse didn't say anything. She bent over her weeding and put her back to us as though we weren't there. "She's thinking of her brother," Ernestine whispered. "The Dauphin. She always does whenever anyone mentions death. I suppose all of them do. At least they've got another prince if they need one."

In all the gossip I'd ever heard about the royal family, I'd never heard anything about Louis Joseph being sick. I said so. "Of course you haven't, it's a secret," whispered Ernestine. "You mustn't tell. He's never been well, and no one thinks he'll live to be king."

Oh. So now I understood Thérèse's cousins' taunts. "It can't be much of a secret," I said, "because her cousins know."

Ernestine frowned. "Everyone in court knows it, of course," she said. "But no one speaks of it publicly, not ever, and no one would breathe a word of it outside of court."

"But the servants must know," I said, thinking of the under-governesses who accompanied Thérèse wherever she went.

"Well, of course, the servants," Ernestine said matter of factly. "They don't count."

Thérèse was near enough to hear all of this, but she didn't say anything. When she finally turned back to us, it was only to show us a flower. We did not speak of the Dauphin.

At noon we dined in Thérèse's rooms. Madame Seamstress had worked miracles, or so it seemed, so that just before the meal I was put into a blue linen dress that matched Thérèse's and Ernestine's. One of the lesser governesses washed our hands and faces, and combed our hair; another scolded us on the state of our shoes, and brought fresh satin slippers for us to wear. Mine were too small, since my feet were bigger than Thérèse's, but I didn't complain.

The grand table was terrifying. Acres of fine white linen covered it, all woven in a damask pattern of flowers and leaves. I fingered the hem, grateful my hands were clean. What I wouldn't give for a shift made of this cloth! "Ernestine," I whispered, "why is there a sheet on the table?"

"It's a tablecloth," she whispered back. "For dining."

"But they'll take it off before we eat," I said. "Won't they? Otherwise we might spill something onto it." Already servants were laying plates and spoons on the beautiful fabric. I winced, wondering if they had washed their hands.

"Of course not," Ernestine whispered back. Thérèse glared at us from across the table, so I closed my mouth, but I couldn't help feeling horrified. All that beautiful cloth! I imagined spilling something on it. I lost my appetite, thinking of the stains.

The plates were made of pottery, like our chamber pots at home, only they seemed much finer than the chamber pots. They were very smooth, and very thin, and painted all over with flowers on a field of blue. The edges were like gold.

"Put that down," Thérèse hissed. "Have you no manners?"

I put the plate down with a thump. "What's it made of?" I asked.

"How should I know?" she asked. "It's only a plate."

The forks and spoons gleamed rosily, and their handles were worked in the most amazing pattern of swirls. I ran my fingertip over the spoon. It couldn't be pewter.

"Ernestine!" hissed Thérèse. "Make her stop that!"

"Please stop," Ernestine whispered, more gently. I put my hand in my lap.

"It's only silver," said Thérèse.

"*Only* silver?" I knew I should keep my mouth shut, but honestly, I couldn't help myself. After all the queen had said about Thérèse being a regular child, I never dreamed she would eat like this.

Thérèse nodded. "We use the gold service only on Sundays," she said. "Maman insists."

I didn't know whether Thérèse meant that the queen insisted they use the gold service once a week, or whether, left to her own choice, Thérèse would eat off gold spoons every day. The second, I guessed.

"It's just dinner," she said. "Just food."

Servants began to bring dishes of food. They went around the table, first to Thérèse, then Madame de Polignac, then Ernestine, then me. My appetite returned in a rush when I saw what was offered. Chicken. Beef in a rich gravy. New peas, and then more meat. A bundle of something that looked like pie crust and smelled spicy and wonderful. Every time I nodded my head, a servant spooned something onto my plate. Soon my plate was piled high, and then–oh, horror!–a drop of sauce did fall off the edge, onto that glittering snow white cloth. I quickly wiped the spot with my finger, then moved the plate onto it so it would not show.

"You must be very hungry," Thérèse said gently. "Did you not eat breakfast before you came?"

I looked up, and saw to my embarrassment that her plate, and Madame de Polignac's and Ernestine's, were all only partially filled. I thought of the large piece of bread I'd had that morning, and the milk, and I sighed and told a lie. "I was so excited to be with you that I could not eat," I said. "I'm very hungry now."

Thérèse smiled. "Then, please, have more."

The first bite of chicken tasted so juicy and wonderful I almost couldn't bring myself to swallow it. I chewed and chewed. The second was as good as the first.

I ate slowly, sitting straight in my chair and copying Thérèse's posture, and the way she held her fork and knife. Madame de Polignac, who hadn't seemed to question my presence at all, said, "And you are Clochette?"

"Yes, madam," I murmured.

"No, she's not," Thérèse said. "Only I may call her that. You must call her Isabelle."

"Very good," Madame de Polignac replied.

I started in on the beef. Then there was something I thought was more chicken, only it wasn't. I wondered what it might be. I didn't want to ask. Instead I said, in what I hoped was a very grand voice, "Do you often eat with the queen?"

Thérèse laughed so that her mouthful of food flew halfway across the table. "Eat with the *queen*!" she said. She covered her face with her napkin and laughed harder. Ernestine laughed, too, and even Madame de Polignac smiled. "Don't you know *anything*?" choked Thérèse.

"I know lots of things," I said through clenched teeth. Though nothing, apparently, about dining at Versailles.

"No, no," she said. "Don't be angry. I just meant–don't you know anything about the court?"

I put down my fork and said nothing.

"The king and queen's midday meal is a ceremony," Madame de Polignac said gently. "Thérèse never eats with them."

"Sometimes other royals do," Thérèse said. "Grown ones, like my uncles or Madame Elizabeth. I might be allowed to watch them, but I don't think I'd like to."

I found I could not swallow another bite of food, even though there was still plenty left on my plate. When servants came around with little cakes and confections, I had to shake my head, even though I'd never seen anything so delicious. "Could I take some home?" I asked.

The servant offering me the tray frowned and swept out of the room. I bit my lip, embarrassed.

"It's only because the servants sell what we don't eat," Thérèse said. "Next time you want something, just put it on your plate, and then put it in your pocket."

I wondered why we'd been served more food than we could possibly eat. "Who do they sell it to?"

"The courtiers, of course," said Thérèse. "We can't afford to feed the whole court, you know."

That night when I got home I fetched a tureen of mutton and parsnip stew from the tavern downstairs, and a loaf of bread from the baker's. Maman poured out the cider, and we sat together with Grand-mère around the table, dipping our bread into our plates of stew. We had just enough for the three of us, and ate every crumb. Our pewter spoons were heavy and dull;

our plates were thick and plain. I saw how the light coming sideways through the window illuminated all the little lines on Maman's tired face.

"Did you have a meal at the palace?" Maman asked.

"Yes." I wondered how I could possibly begin to describe it.

"Good," Maman said. "Then you can't be very hungry. Grand-mère and I will split the rest of the stew." She scraped the last bits from the tureen onto her plate, and wiped out the tureen with a crust of bread.

I couldn't describe it, I decided. There was no possible place to begin.

Chapter Six

"How did Her Majesty like the lace?" Grand-mère asked as I was climbing into bed beside her that night.

"What lace?" I saw something small scuttle beneath the sheet and I dove after it, crushing the little bug between my fingertips. I had forgotten all about the lace I was supposed to have given to the queen.

Grand-mère clouted my head to help me remember. "The lace you left with this morning. You did give it to Her Majesty, didn't you?"

"Not in person," I said carefully. I couldn't admit that I'd lost the package.

"Worthless girl! I suppose you left it with a servant, didn't you?"

I bit my lip. "I'm sure it will get to Her Majesty."

Grand-mère clouted me again. "Silly fool," she said. "How do you know that servant didn't keep it for herself? Tomorrow you must hand it to her in person."

"The queen isn't always with Thérèse," I said, "and I can't make them let me see her. I have to do what Thérèse wants."

"You must do better," Grand-mère insisted, "else we might as well keep you working here at home."

In the morning Grand-mère scrubbed my face hard and sent me back to the palace with another paper package of lace in my hands. "Hold on to it until you can give it to the queen herself," she said. "From your hands to hers."

I hesitated a little before knocking on the door to Thérèse's rooms. She had not specifically said that she wanted me today. But when she saw me, she grinned and said, "Oh, good morning, Clochette," and told me to change my clothes quickly. I put my parcel on the table and shimmied out of my dress into the one set out for me on a chair in the corner of the room. Today we were all wearing pale blue, with an underskirt trimmed with narrow cotton lace that I examined carefully. It was bobbin lace, not needle lace like my family made, and I liked my own lace better.

When I returned to the table, Thérèse had unwrapped the package and was examining the lace I'd brought, in the same way I had examined the dress.

"Did you make this?" she demanded.

"No," I said. I took it from her. "My grandmother did. Her wrappings are finer than my mother's, because my mother's hands hurt her these days."

"Could you make something like it?" Thérèse asked.

I nodded. "It's for the queen," I said. "Grand-mère told me to give it to your mother."

Thérèse frowned. "A sample," she said. "Your Grand-mère wants the queen my mother to buy lace from you. Right?"

"Yes," I said. "But I shall not say so. I shall tell the queen your mother that it is a gift."

Thérèse said, "It can't matter to you whether my mother buys your lace or not."

I had trouble swallowing my amazement. "Of course it does," I said. "Everyone desires royal patronage. If we sell–" Thérèse's face was darkening now. I tried to say the truth without upsetting her. "We are lacemakers. It's what we do, how we earn our bread. If we don't sell lace, we don't eat. So of course we want to sell it–to the queen or to anyone else."

Thérèse still frowned. "You are too young to earn anything," she said. "Children do not work."

"But Thérèse, of course I work," I said. "I earn my keep. I learned to make lace years ago. My brother became a full-time stable lad when he was eight. Pierre, the candle boy, and the servants in the kitchen–" Children worked hard all through Versailles. Was Thérèse blind?

"That is ridiculous," Thérèse said. "Certainly some peasant children must work, but not my friends. Not you. Not Ernestine." Behind Thérèse's back, I saw Ernestine raise her eyebrows slightly, as though she disagreed. Then she shook her head at me, the tiniest bit. Perhaps Ernestine and I had more in common than I'd thought.

"You *don't* work," Thérèse said. "You come here to play with me because I want you to, and because you want to come. It is *not* a job."

"I love coming here," I said earnestly. "I love being with you."

"Your Grand-mère makes lace," she continued. "Your mother does. Not you." She lifted her chin and stared straight at me.

I stared straight back. "My Grand-mère made this lace," I said, touching the parcel. "She wishes me to give it to your mother the queen."

Thérèse nodded. "Very well." She looked somewhat pleased, as though she thought she had won an admission from me. But I knew I had not budged very far. She could not make me say that I did not make lace. Grand-mère and Maman would never let me forget, not as long as I went home to them every night. I rubbed the calluses on my fingertips.

Thérèse flicked a sullen glance at Ernestine, and Ernestine flicked one back. "We have a riding lesson this morning," Thérèse said. "Ernestine doesn't like it. She's afraid of horses."

"I am not," cried Ernestine. "Only Jacques, and you make me ride him."

"He's nothing but a pony," Thérèse spat back. "Nothing to be afraid of." She folded my piece of lace and tied the paper back around it. "I suppose you're frightened too," she said.

"I have told you already that I'm not."

"He's a devil pony–" muttered Ernestine.

"And," cut in Thérèse, ignoring her, "we want to meet this brother of yours."

"He lives at the stables," I said. "He's there whenever we want him."

Thérèse smiled. "We may as well go see my mother right now," she said. "We will give her your lace and then we'll ride. Afterward we can see your brother."

I was so pleased I wouldn't have to lie to Grand-mère that I put my hand around Ernestine's waist. "I'll ride the devil pony," I said.

I walked to the big door that led to the marble hallway, but Thérèse laughed and motioned me to the side of the room. "We only use that for public walking," she said. "For going to chapel, or something like that." She nodded at one of the servants, who pressed a small lever hidden in the carved molding on the wall, and opened a door set so flush into the paneling that I hadn't noticed it was there.

Thérèse laughed again at my surprise. "It's the back hallway," she said. "The servants use it. So do I. So does anyone who doesn't want to be looked at."

This hallway was small and plain, with no carvings or marble, but, like the main hall, it was lit with branch after branch of long white candles. We passed many closed doors, and even staircases going both up and down. Servants hurried all around us, carrying slop jars and firewood and buckets of water. Finally Thérèse stopped. "Maman's bedchamber," she said. "Soon she will get dressed."

The queen was sitting on a pretty chair, sipping tea from a china cup. She wore a loose gown and her hair fell all around her shoulders. When she saw us, she smiled joyfully and got up to embrace us. Several of her ladies had been sitting in a cluster around her, but when she got up, they also jumped to their feet. Only after the queen had sat down, and Thérèse as well, did they resume their seats.

"How wonderful of you to visit me!" said the queen.

"Clochette has brought you a present," said Thérèse.

"I'm Clochette," I added. "It's what Thérèse calls me."

"A pet name," Thérèse said happily. "She likes it."

The queen had a large book open on the dressing table in front of her. Small pieces of cloth were pasted onto its open pages. She slid a long pin into one of the pieces, then gravely handed the book to a lady, who bowed and backed out of the room. "It's my wardrobe book," she said, smiling at my puzzlement. "It has swatches from all my dresses in it. Every morning

I choose the gowns for the day, and that way my ladies know which gowns to bring me."

Gowns? I thought. *More than one gown, every day?* And the book had been so thick–the queen must have had hundreds of dresses. I longed to see them.

"So?" said the queen.

"Give her the package," prompted Thérèse.

I knelt and laid the little parcel in the queen's hands. "I told Your Majesty that I would make you a gift of lace," I said, remembering what I had said to her in the hall.

The queen opened it and spread it out on her dressing table. "And so you have kept your promise," she said. "Do you always keep promises?"

I could not think of another promise I had made to anyone. "Yes," I said. "I always, always do."

Several more ladies walked into the room. Some of them brought folding chairs, which they began to set up in long rows. The queen sighed. "Time for me to be dressed," she said. She kissed Thérèse, and patted me and Ernestine. "Have a lovely day, my dears."

Thérèse and Ernestine got up to leave. I followed them reluctantly. "Do you think she liked the lace?"

Thérèse shrugged. "Of course. Why shouldn't she?"

"She didn't say so."

"Why should she say so? She has plenty of lace."

I looked back into the room as we disappeared through another paneled door. The queen's ladies-in-waiting all stood before her in a long line. They were passing some sort of shift or undergarment down the line, from one person to the next. "What are they doing?"

"Dressing the queen," Thérèse said impatiently. "What do you think?"

"Does it take that many people?"

Thérèse rolled her eyes. "It's part of the court. The queen gets dressed, the queen eats dinner, the queen undresses and goes to bed. Anyone who wishes may take part. They pass my mother's garments up the line in order of rank, and the most important lady there gets to put them into my mother's hands."

"Anyone who wishes?"

"Any noble," Thérèse said. "Any person important enough to be allowed into my mother's rooms."

I had just been allowed into the queen's rooms.

Thérèse must have guessed what I was thinking, because she smiled serenely and said, "You are important when you are with me. But we don't want to help my mother get dressed."

"No," I agreed. "That would be awful." I had felt shy about changing my dress in the corner of Thérèse's room, and I had kept my shift on and had not had anyone actually watching.

Thérèse nodded. "Very boring," she said. "It takes an hour. Sometimes more, if lots of ladies come. My mother dislikes it."

"Why does she do it, then?"

"She *has* to, silly. She's the queen."

For our riding lesson we did not go to the stables as I'd expected. Instead we walked out into the park, and Thérèse's riding master brought the ponies to us. He was a very grand man, with shiny black boots and a large puffy wig. He rode a big bay horse. For the three of us there were three ponies in sidesaddles, a fat gray, a sleepy-looking bay, and a grumpy little chestnut that I was sure must be the devil pony, Jacques.

I was right. "If Madame would please to take Jacques," the riding master said, in a formal clipped voice.

"No," Thérèse said coolly. "I'll have Snowball, please."

I reached to pat Jacques, but he moved away. "I said I'd ride him," I said.

The riding master looked down his long nose at me. If we'd met on the streets of Versailles, he would have been too grand to even glance my way. I would not have merited one moment of his attention. "As miss prefers," he said politely.

"Miss Isabelle Bonnard," Thérèse said. "You must call her Miss Isabelle."

The man did not even blink. "As Miss Isabelle prefers," he said. "Has Miss Isabelle ever sat a horse before?"

"Sir, I have not," I said.

The riding master made some movement with his hand, and a pair of boys I had not noticed before came forward. They reminded me of George; I knew they must be grooms. One of them went to Ernestine and offered his cupped hands to lift her into the saddle of the little bay pony. The other took Jacques's reins from the servant holding them, and put them over the pony's head. "If Miss Isabelle would hold the reins, then step into my hands," he said.

Close up the pony seemed bigger. He tossed his head and the groom yanked hard on the rein. "Don't be afraid," the groom said to me. "I will not let him off the leading rein."

I was afraid, but I didn't want to show it. The riding master himself put Thérèse into the saddle. She gathered up the reins and settled her bottom more firmly in the saddle. I could see that she knew exactly what to do. Ernestine looked less certain.

She leaned forward, and when her pony began to move, she snatched at the reins with her hands. Anyone could see that the pony didn't like it. The pony began to prance.

My groom kept Jacques on a short lead. I thrust my left foot into the stirrup and arranged my right thigh over the hook of the saddle as the groom directed me to do. The skirt of my dress seemed exactly suited for riding. When I said so, the groom looked impassive. Ernestine giggled. "It's a riding habit, of course," she said. "Didn't you know?"

How could I have known? There were thousands of things I didn't know.

I tried to ride the opposite of Ernestine, to sit straight and hold the reins softly. My groom clucked and Jacques stepped forward in a swinging walk. "Very nice," the riding master said. "Relax, so that you move with him. Don't bounce."

We rode down one of the long promenades, the riding master up front with Thérèse, and Ernestine and I side by side behind them, the grooms walking with us.

All around us the courtiers of Versailles were taking the morning air. We rode down the side of the grand canal, where men in strange costumes poled long boats lazily back and forth. We rode past other men and women on horseback. Most of them bowed to Thérèse. Some of them bowed to all three of us. "They can't tell which the princess is," I whispered to Ernestine. It astonished me, that I could be mistaken for a princess.

Ernestine nodded without looking at me. All her attention was fixed on her sleepy-looking pony. I loved the back and forth sway of Jacques's hips and the soft pressure of his mouth on the reins. At the same time I couldn't help but stare at the court ladies who passed us. Their gowns were more elaborate than any I'd seen so far. We passed one woman whose rose pink skirts were so wide she could barely walk against the moderate wind. She looked like the kite George had made for me long ago, only upside down, wide at the bottom with the long ribbons of her headdress fluttering like a kite's tail.

Jacques sidled away from the woman as we walked past her. The woman put her hands on her panniers and swore softly under her breath. She wore lace gloves and ribbons around her wrists. Her skin was white as milk, and so was her towering powdered hair.

The breeze had been ticklish, but suddenly it blew hard. It blew the fancy woman's hair straight off her head.

Jacques leaped. I lurched forward. My groom yelled and let go of the lead. The hair–a wig, I realized, a giant powdered wig, with ribbons and flowers stuck in it–blew rolling down the promenade, and Jacques whirled and bucked and ran.

On the first leap I let go of the reins and grabbed Jacques's mane with both my hands. As he whirled, I lost my balance, and my foot came out of the stirrup. My skirt caught on the top of the saddle and I hung off the pony's bouncing side, suspended only from my hands and the fabric of my skirt. I screamed. If I let go, and my skirt stayed caught, I would be dragged.

All I could see was Jacques's flying mane, and my fingers clutching it. His hooves pounded on the paving stones. I heard shouts and more hoofbeats. Jacques ran and ran. My skirt began to tear. "Hold on!" I heard someone yell. "Hold on!"

Jacques swerved around a corner. I heard shouts and curses from people jumping out of his way. Suddenly he began to slide, his hooves skidding out from under him on the slick stones. The pony and I fell together. The weight of his body against my side was the last thing I knew before my head hit the ground, and everything went black.

When I opened my eyes, I still could not see. Everything was black and for a moment I thought I must be blind. I sat up in panic, crying out. A wave of pain hit my head as though someone had swung a hammer against my skull. I fell back in agony, against something soft. A pillow. I was in a bed. I could see dim shapes now, dark curtains wavering softly around windows. I was not blind. It was night.

"Bella!" hissed a voice near my head. "Bella, don't scream! Are you all right?"

"George!" Always, always, George would save me.

"Yes, it's me. For heaven's sake don't scream anymore! You'll wake up everyone. Are you okay? You've been snoring like a soldier for hours. That quack of a court physician wanted to bleed you, but Madame Royale wouldn't let him."

I wanted to sit up, but my head hurt too much to move. I was horribly thirsty, but couldn't figure out how to ask for water. Speaking seemed like too much of an effort.

From across the room I heard a clear familiar voice say, "A candle, please." Someone lit Thérèse a candle. She held it up and walked toward us, her long white nightgown trailing along the floor. If I were dead, in heaven, she would be an angel. But if I were dead, surely my head couldn't hurt so much.

"She's awake?" Thérèse asked George.

"Yes, but she's not speaking."

"I expect she's thirsty. Give her some water."

George poured water from a nearby pitcher into a mug, and held it to my lips. He didn't lift my head high enough, and water poured down the sides of my face and soaked the pillow. "Clumsy!" Thérèse scolded. "Where is Madame de Polignac? Someone else do it!"

An undergoverness, a plump matronly woman, rose from her pallet near the fire. She lifted my head gently in her arms and held the mug of water to my lips. "Thank you," I whispered. The woman turned my pillow so that I no longer had to lie on the damp spot. She straightened my sheets and wiped my face, and went away.

I whispered to Thérèse, "Are there always so many people here at night?"

Thérèse ignored the question. "Are you hurt much?"

"My head hurts very much," I whispered. "I'm so tired."

"Anything else? The pony fell on you, you know, but the physician didn't think you'd broken any bones. Can you move your fingers and toes?"

I ached everywhere, but I could move my fingers and toes. I didn't feel sharp pains anywhere except in my head. I said so.

George still held my hand. "I had them find your brother for you," Thérèse said. "I thought you would wish it."

"I'll go tell Maman you've woken," George said. "She'll be relieved." He kissed my cheek, bowed to Thérèse, and slipped away.

Thérèse pulled one of the room's little chairs to my bedside. My eyes had grown used to the darkness and I saw where I was now, in a little bed next to Thérèse's larger one. "Shall I sit up with you?" Thérèse said. "The only good part of being sick in bed is having someone sit up with you. When I am very sick, my mother comes to sit up with me. She stays with me all night, sometimes. She's always sitting up with my brother the Dauphin."

I wanted my own mother. I was glad enough to have Thérèse beside me, but I wished for my mother as well. My headache made it so hard to speak that I couldn't say so. Tears rolled down my cheeks.

"Don't worry," Thérèse said softly. "I'm here."

I want Maman, I thought. But before I could make myself say so, I fell asleep.

Chapter Seven

I stayed two weeks in that bed in Thérèse's bedchamber, my head hurting dreadfully, but a little less every day. In that time, without realizing it, I learned to be a member of the court.

In the morning the servants who slept in Thérèse's rooms woke first. They summoned other servants, who brought wood to build up the fire, and swept ashes away, and carried out the chamber pots. Every servant had a particular job; no servant would have dreamed of doing a job that belonged to someone else. If the fire needed tending, but none of the servants who tended it were on hand, the fire could go right out while the undergovernesses and the servants in charge of the wardrobe shivered and fussed. The first time this happened I tried to get out of bed myself, to throw another log on and jab the embers with a poker. But anytime I got to my feet, my head swirled so that I nearly fell down.

Thérèse saw me and came running. "What are you doing? You are not well!"

"I'll show you how to poke up that fire," I said. "It's not difficult." I really could not stand, and I allowed one of the undergovernesses to help me lie back down. "I'll tell you how to do it," I said to Thérèse. "Take that poker there–"

"You expect me to build up a fire?" Thérèse's concern vanished and her eyes blazed with anger. "You're commanding me?"

The undergoverness put her hand to my head. "Poor thing must be delirious," she said. "Quite out of her mind."

Thérèse's expression softened as quickly as it had gone hard. "Poor Clochette. You must summon the physicians again."

I wanted to say that of course I was not delirious, that Thérèse was more than capable of wielding a poker, and that if the queen truly wanted Thérèse to act like a normal child, she should allow her to at least take action to keep herself warm. I understood that Thérèse must not empty chamber pots, but surely she could put wood onto the fire? Or if not her, then one of the undergovernesses? The rooms teemed with servants.

I wanted to say all that, but I fell asleep before I could murmur a word. I fell asleep all the time; I dropped off entirely without warning.

When I woke hours later, the fire was blazing brightly, and the room seemed overhot. Thérèse and Ernestine were gone. A woman–the matronly servant who'd brought me water–sat by my side. She brought me a cup of tea to drink now, and wiped my forehead with a damp cloth. "The fire people came," I said.

The woman smacked her lips nervously. "My Jenny is scullery maid here in the morning, and does up the fires," she said, after a pause. "She does her best, miss, truly. She's a good girl. But it's a long way from these rooms to the woodpiles, and to where she dumps the ashes."

"I'm sure it is," I said. "I only thought that–"

"I know what you thought, miss," the woman said, "but please, don't think it again. Folks must keep their proper station. Shall I get you some sugar for your tea?"

I nodded. I never had sugar at home–how could I, with what it cost?–and I loved it.

"How old is your Jenny?"

"She's seven, miss. She's a strong, good girl."

Every morning when Thérèse woke, someone brought her a cup of chocolate, which she drank sitting up in bed. They brought me chocolate too. I'd never drunk any before, and at first it was hard to get used to the taste, chalky and thick, only a little bit sweet.

Another servant brought in Thérèse's dress, and the matching one for Ernestine, and laid them out, and helped Thérèse to dress. Her clothes were always simple, though of fine fabric and well made. On mornings when she rode, she wore a riding habit.

I did not dress. I was helped out of bed and onto the chamber pot, and then (my head spinning, pounding) I was helped to a chair while my bed was made up with fresh sheets. My pillows were plumped, and then someone helped me change into a new nightgown, and combed my hair. At Thérèse's insistence, I even washed my face. She washed her face every single day, her hands before every meal, and had a hot bath once a week as well. It made the servants grumble, but I noticed that Thérèse had many fewer fleas than most of the courtiers. "My mother insists on it," she told me. "She is Austrian, you know, and the Austrian court is cleaner than the French."

I had fleas, of course. No one I knew bathed regularly. I did not see why Thérèse fussed so much about the bugs, though of course it would be pleasant not to itch.

Ernestine arrived in time for breakfast. Then most mornings the governesses taught them, in the big room adjoining the bedroom. Both Thérèse and Ernestine could read and write in French and Latin. They also studied geography, history, music, and mathematics.

On my first full day of lying in bed, Thérèse came in midmorning to check on me. "I brought you a book," she said, "so you wouldn't be so bored."

"I can't read," I whispered. Her voice was so loud, it made my head pound more.

"Oh, your head is still hurting you!" Thérèse laid the book aside and put her small hand to my forehead.

My head hurt, of course, but that was not what I'd meant. Ernestine understood. "I think she doesn't know how to read," she whispered to Thérèse.

Thérèse looked shocked. "Oh, poor Clochette! Then I will send you a governess to teach you." But when the governess came, I was already nearly asleep. The woman looked at me, picked up the book, and began, softly and slowly, to read it aloud. I fell sound asleep without comprehending a word.

The servants called me Miss Isabelle. Thérèse allowed only herself and Ernestine to call me Clochette.

George came to me every day and sometimes stayed as long as half an hour beside my bed. He was shy around Thérèse and tried to come when he thought she and Ernestine were most likely to be outdoors. He was sitting on the stool pulled close to my pillow one fine afternoon, and I was telling him that I felt much better, and had walked partway across the room that morning, when one of the side panel doors into the room opened, and in came the king. I recognized him right away, though I hadn't spoken to him before.

George dropped to his knee in an instant, swept off his hat, and put his gaze to the floor. I wasn't sure what to do. It was true I'd walked partway across the floor in the morning, but it was also true that the effort had exhausted me, that I'd nearly collapsed, and that only prompt action from one of the governesses had gotten me safely back to the bed. Now my dizziness had returned. If I got up from bed, I wouldn't bow to the king, I would faint dead at his feet. Still, there must be some proper way to make reverence to a king, even when one was wearing nothing but a nightgown and lying flat in bed.

"Sire," I whispered, and tried to bob my head.

If the king expected more, he didn't show it. He swept the skirts of his coat aside and sat upon George's stool. "So you are my daughter's little friend," he said. "The one that fell off the pony."

"Yes, Sire," I said. "I am not yet a good rider."

I had to admit that the king did not look much like a king. He wore his fine clothes awkwardly, as though he were uncomfortable in them. His face was thick, his hair untidy, and his eyes small. He squinted when he spoke to me. But my answer made him smile, and when he smiled he looked kind.

"Not yet!" he said. "Do you wish to become a rider, then?"

I had not thought much about it. "I think so," I said slowly. "I was only afraid when the pony ran, and only then because my skirt got caught."

"Well, well," he said. "I look forward to the day when my daughter goes hunting with me. Perhaps you will join us."

"Thank you, Sire," I said. "I should like that."

"And what of the pony, eh? The bad Jacques? Should he be fed to my hounds, for what he did?"

"For throwing me, Sire?" Surely he wasn't serious!

It appeared that he was, however, for he said, without jesting at all, "All useless horses are slaughtered and fed to the hounds. If one of my hunters breaks its leg, for example. That is what hounds eat."

"It wasn't Jacques's fault," I said. "It was that lady in the pink dress. She scared him when her wig blew off. That wig was enough to scare anyone."

The king seemed amused. "All right, then," he said. "We'll make him a cart pony, for the kitchens. He can't harm you or my daughter there." He fished around inside one of his coat pockets and drew out a small box. "Perhaps you might like this," he said. He handed it to me and then left, without a backward glance or another word. He used the side door again, the one that led to the servants' back hallway.

All this time George had knelt silently beside the king. Now he raised his face and looked at me in awe. "Good God, Bella, you were talking to the *king*!" he said.

"He seemed kind," I said. "He wasn't frightening."

"But he's the king!"

"People are allowed to speak to the king," I said.

"Not regular people," George insisted. "Only nobles, and courtiers, and–you spoke to him like he was the curate, or the butcher–or some normal person!" He seemed truly shaken. I was not shaken at all.

"He's Thérèse's father," I said.

"Thérèse is Madame Royale!" When I didn't reply, George went on, "I have worked for the marquis for six years and have never once spoken to him. How could I? I'm nobody. And the marquis–the marquis is nobody, compared to the king!"

"You're not nobody."

"Bella, I am. I know it. You must know it too."

"I am not nobody," I said. George looked horrified.

"You are," he whispered. "Please don't forget that you are. It would be so dangerous for you to forget."

But I wasn't nobody. I was Thérèse's friend Clochette. Lying there, on silk sheets in a room with a painted ceiling and gilded walls, I couldn't find anything to say to bridge the distance that had suddenly opened between my brother and me.

When Thérèse and Ernestine returned from the gardens, I showed them the little box. Inside was a small key that would lock it. Thérèse examined the box carefully, then returned it to me with a fond smile. "Papa makes them," she said. "I have several."

"The king of France makes boxes?"

"He makes locks," she said. "Locks are what he loves. He only makes boxes to have something to lock."

That night I awoke to snarling shrieks. It was rats fighting in the corner. They came out at night to scavenge bits of food and bones the dogs left behind. Normally they didn't wake me, but this time their fight was savage, their screams nearly human. After a while I heard a thud as one of the servants threw something at them. The snarls subsided, then started again.

I sat up in bed, wondering if I should throw something too. I didn't really want to lose my pillow to a rat. I was reaching for the hairbrush on the table nearby when I heard another sound that made me freeze.

Sobs. Quiet, muffled sobs. "Thérèse?" I whispered.

The sobs stopped abruptly. I climbed out of bed, steadied myself for a moment, then crept to her bed and pushed back the hangings around it. "It's just rats," I said.

Thérèse rolled over and pulled her pillow away from her face. In the moonlight I could see streaks of tears running down her face. "I know," she said, "but I don't like them."

"They won't climb onto the beds. Will they?" Perhaps the palace rats were bolder than the ones at home.

Thérèse shuddered. "Sometimes."

"Scoot over." She moved to the other side of the bed. I climbed in beside her and put my arms around her. She held herself perfectly stiff. "Now you are safe," I said. "I won't let the rats hurt you. You don't have to be afraid."

"I am one of the Children of France," she replied. "I am never afraid." But she pressed her face to my shoulder and let her body relax, and a few moments later she was asleep.

I didn't sleep well. Perhaps I had finally slept too much during the day. I listened to Thérèse breathing and the rats screaming and the old woman who slept near the fireplace snoring. I wanted my mother so much, I ached. I dozed a bit, and was wide awake when the servants came with chocolate for Thérèse and me.

"Good morning, Clochette," Thérèse said with a sleepy smile. She accepted her chocolate and sipped it. "Did you sleep well?"

"No," I said. "I miss my mother. I have seen you and Ernestine and George every day, and the queen twice, and even the king, but I miss my mother and I want to see her face."

Thérèse nodded. "Of course! I should have thought of that. I will send for her immediately, and she will come."

Chapter Eight

I waited so happily. One of the servants propped me up on a pile of pillows and washed my face and hands. Another carefully combed my hair, and tied it back with a wide silk ribbon. My hair had been combed so much while I was at the palace that it was free of fleas and nits; Thérèse was right, it really did feel better. With my grooming complete, I lay back with a happy sigh and watched the servants put the room to rights, building up the fire, clearing away the clutter and the breakfast things. When the door to the big hallway opened, I turned my face toward it with a wide smile, but it was only Louis Charles, Thérèse's three-year-old brother, with his nurse.

"Chette!" he said, beaming at me. His rooms adjoined Thérèse's, and he often came in to play.

"Good morning, little man," I said.

Because he was only three, he couldn't talk properly, but I had learned to understand him pretty well. Now he said something that sounded like "Head better?" and I said, "Much better, thank you. I'm waiting for my maman."

"Maman!" he cried, wheeling around as though expecting to see the queen.

"No, not your maman. My maman. I'm waiting. Come, sit here." I patted the mattress beside me. He came and perched himself on the edge of the feather bed, and swung his feet. Thérèse ran in with one of the queen's pug dogs, and the prince laughed so hard at it that she put the pug dog on my bed too. She found an old bone for the dog to chew. Then she sat beside her brother and tickled him, and he giggled until neither Thérèse nor I could stop laughing.

I didn't see my mother walk into the room. She must have stood for a few minutes in the corner, watching me play and laugh with the Children of France. One of the servants finally tapped my shoulder, and I looked up to see my little mother leaning on her walking stick, her face pale and her eyes full of an expression I had never seen before.

"Oh, Maman!" I cried. The look of shock slowly faded from her face, replaced by an artificial smile. She hobbled slowly toward us. I had never noticed before how shabbily my mother dressed, or how lined and old her face seemed, or how plain her hair, put up simply on her head without powder or ribbons or ornaments. She looked more slovenly than the merest servant, than Jenny, the girl who swept out the fire in the morning. I swallowed, and tried not to feel ashamed. What would Thérèse think? "I missed you, Maman," I said.

Thérèse slid off the bed, pushed the dog down, and gathered her brother in her arms. "Thérèse, this is my maman," I said. "Maman, Madame Royale and Monsieur the Duke of Normandy."

Maman tried to curtsy, but her knees could not do it. Her walking stick trembled so that it was painful to watch. "Oh, please don't!" Thérèse said. She called for a chair to be brought for my mother to sit in. Then, smiling at me, she took Charles out to the terrace to play.

Maman refused to sit in the chair. "It's too fine," she said. "What if I break it?"

I couldn't bear to see her standing when I knew how her knees hurt. "It's only a chair," I said. "Sit down."

"Only a chair! Merciful heavens, Isabelle! Look at it! We couldn't buy such a chair if we sold everything we owned to pay for it."

The chair was carved all over, back and legs; the seat cushions were silk damask and every inch of the frame had been gilded. For certain it was an expensive chair. But the pug dog sat on it and chewed his bones and drooled, and I could see marks on the chair's legs that had come from either the dog's teeth or Charles being careless with his toys. No one treasured that chair. "Maman," I said, "it's the plainest chair they have here. Please sit down."

She sat, but she was not easy. I had expected her to fuss over me, and pat my forehead, and kiss me and say how glad she was that I was better. Instead she held herself away, and stared at me as though I were a changeling. "They dress you very fine," she said.

"It's only a nightgown, Maman."

She sniffed, and I hoped she was noticing the perfume in my hair. "I never imagined," she said, "that the palace could smell so bad."

The palace stank. "One grows used to it," I said. Then I realized how insufferable I sounded. "Oh, Maman," I said, "please don't look at me like this. I've missed you so much! How are you? How–how is Grand-mère?"

Maman's forehead creased. "We're keeping up with the

work," she said. "Mostly because there's been very little work to do. And my hands–" She spread them out. I could see how red and swollen they were. "If you had to have such an accident, I suppose it's lucky you had it here. We couldn't have paid for a doctor at home."

"I've missed you," I whispered.

"George tells me how you are doing," she said. "He comes home after he visits you here. He said you're improving, said you've been walking around." She eyed my pile of pillows.

"I've walked a little," I said. "I am getting better, but my head still hurts all the time." Now I was whining, and I hated myself for it. Maman hurt all the time, and didn't complain. I sounded like Grand-mère.

Maman leaned forward and kissed me. Her lips were featherlight against my cheek. "Get well soon, and come home," she said. "We need you there." She looked around the room as if it frightened her. "Come home, Isabelle. We don't belong at this palace. I'll never come here again."

Chapter Nine

After she left, Thérèse bounced in. "Was it wonderful?" she asked. "Seeing your maman? Oh–you're crying!" She hurried to get me a handkerchief. "I'm sorry," she said, watching as I wiped my eyes. "I used to cry too when I wanted my mother. Mostly I don't anymore."

I was not crying because Maman was gone. I was crying because she looked so different–because she had changed, or rather, I had. I wanted Maman and me to be the same, but instead of going back to my old self I wanted her to be as I was now.

"What did you think of her?" I asked.

Thérèse looked puzzled. "Why would I think of her? She's your maman, what you wanted. Right?"

Thérèse might be blind, I thought, *but she isn't a snob.* She was simply royal to her bones.

"I fetched her for you," Thérèse said. "Can you bear to do something with me now? Is your head better enough? Ernestine stayed home for her mother today, and my mother"–she made a face–"my mother is off at the Trianon, rehearsing one of her plays. And it's raining. Can you play chess?"

I struggled to sit up higher. "I can learn," I said.

That night I felt lonelier than ever, and the screams of the rats fighting in the night were almost impossible to endure. My head ached from tiredness, but I couldn't sleep. I stared at the low glow from the embers in the fireplace. "Clochette?" Thérèse whispered.

"Yes?" I whispered back.

"I just wondered," she said. "I thought you were awake."

"Are you frightened?" I asked.

After a pause she said, "The rats make such awful noise."

I got up and climbed into her bed beside her. She huddled against me. After a few moments she said, "Your mother loves you. She came as soon as she was asked."

"She didn't want to come," I said. I felt bitter. "She says she's not coming back."

Thérèse sighed. "I had been hoping you could stay here with me forever, but I know you must go home. Not yet, not until you are better, but sometime."

Tears rolled down my cheeks. My accident had turned me into someone who cried all the time.

Rats squealed and shrieked. Thérèse shuddered. "Do you have a sister?" she whispered.

"No," I said. "No one but George, Maman, and Grand-mère. Maman's parents are dead. Grand-mère was Papa's mother, and he her only son."

There was a pause. The servant sleeping on the floor by the fire rolled over, and began to snore. How the servants could ignore the rats, I couldn't imagine. "I had a sister," Thérèse whispered. "We all loved her. She didn't live very long."

"I remember," I said.

"My mother has family all over Europe. Her mother was the

empress of Austria! And Maman was her fifteenth child, and all but two lived to be married. Imagine that! I have an uncle who is the emperor of Austria, and another who will be emperor if he dies, and an aunt who is queen of Naples. Maman says that even if all this talk of revolution goes anywhere, we will always be safe, because we are related to so many heads of state."

I had never heard of any talk of revolution. I wasn't even sure what she meant. I didn't ask. Her voice soothed me; as my headache eased, I grew sleepier. "Your father has brothers too," I said. "And a sister, Madame Elizabeth."

"Pooh! My uncles are worthless. And their sniveling dirty little wives, and my horrible cousins. My aunt Elizabeth, now, I do love her."

I had met Madame Elizabeth. She was younger than the queen, not married, and very beautiful. She seemed to love everyone.

The wind changed directions. A gust of foul-smelling air wafted into the room. I coughed. "The palace gets worse as the weather improves," Thérèse said quietly. "Maman says such putrid air isn't healthy. When it gets hot, midsummer, we go to the summer palace at Saint-Cloud. Perhaps you may come too."

"I would like it more than anything," I said.

"Maman will say yes," Thérèse said. "I am sure."

A week later I could walk back and forth across Thérèse's rooms without stumbling or coming near to faint. When Thérèse and Ernestine returned from chapel, I told them I must go home. "But you are not nearly well enough," Thérèse said. "Your head still aches. You know it does."

Ernestine's face was blotched with tears. Every day she lit candles in the chapel for her mother, who grew more and more sick. "I must go," I said. A nightmare had woken me. I was beginning to think I'd never sleep soundly at the palace again. "Something's wrong at home. I don't know what. I must be there." George had gone away to Paris with the marquis, and I hadn't seen him for several days. Maman, true to her word, had not come back. Yet I knew something was wrong. My stomach felt tight and queer.

Thérèse nodded. "I will order you a carriage," she said. "You aren't strong enough to walk so far."

I wanted to be strong with all my might, but my will couldn't overpower my frail body. Even the jolts of the carriage seemed tiring, and when the footman helped me out at the stairs leading to our apartment, my legs trembled and I nearly fell. With great dignity the footman carried me up to our door. I stood for a moment gathering my breath. The royal carriage rolled away. I went inside.

The fire had gone out. Light streamed through the open windows into the untidy room, showing crumbs on the table, unwashed dishes, unmade beds. A filled chamber pot left such a stench that if I closed my eyes, I would think I was back at Versailles. Grandmère and Maman were at their chairs by the windows, making lace. For a moment, before they looked up at me, everything seemed so perfectly normal, except for the squalor, that I thought my intuition had been wrong. Then Maman turned worried eyes to me, and I knew that something truly was wrong.

"Isabelle! Thank God! We need you." She got up, grabbed her stick, and hobbled to my side.

"Maman, I'm sorry. I'm still so weak–" I looked at the chamber pot in despair. "It's so heavy, I don't know if I can–"

Maman brushed that aside. "Forget the pot, there's another under the bed we can use. Get your needle, Isabelle. You'll see it's a good thing we trained you well."

Maman could tell I was still wobbly. She helped me push the bed so it would sit in a pool of light, and let me stretch my legs out and prop my shoulders against the headboard. She gave me a strip of linen marked with the ground lines for a piece a lace. She gave me needle and thread. "Do your best work, now, and quickly. The man comes every day to complain, and if we don't have something to show him, he'll cancel the order. If he cancels the order, we won't be able to pay for the thread. Then we won't eat. You see how it is?"

I looked at Grand-mère. Her hands moved repetitively in the light by the window. Her lips moved too, though soundlessly. Then I realized with a chill that Grand-mère wasn't holding a needle. She was tying the thread into knots with her hands.

"Some sort of stroke," Maman whispered. "She can't talk. Her hands aren't working well. Nor her brain, I think. She'll twist that piece of thread all day long."

Grand-mère, the monster of my childhood. I watched her warily, not trusting the transformation. She didn't so much as look at me.

"Please hurry," Maman whispered. "Get something started. I have been trying, but with my hands so bad–this is the best I can do." She showed me the piece she was working on. The twists were looser than they should be, and the knots uneven. I had done better work when I was six years old. Grand-mère and Maman had done better work always.

Maman brought me a cup of tea. I sipped it, then started work. Straw poked out of holes in the mattress cover and scratched my legs. I felt a flea jump from the mattress to my leg. I was back to wearing my homemade gown, the one I had worn to the palace weeks ago. I had gained weight and the dress pulled uncomfortably across my shoulders. I tugged at the tight fabric and wished for my palace nightgowns, so soft and trimmed with lace. "Can't we get someone to empty that chamber pot?" I said. The stench made it difficult to breathe.

"Who?" Maman said. "We have here you, and me. You need to start working, and if I try I will drop it down the stairs."

I swung my legs to the floor. "I'll do it," I said. "If I just get rid of it, the air–"

Maman whirled around, furious. "Get to work!" she said. "Lazy girl! We don't have time for this nonsense!"

"I'm not–"

Her glare cut me off. Meek Maman, gentle Maman, who for years had been the only slight buffer between Grand-mère and me, now seemed to have taken on Grand-mère's personality. She hounded me throughout the morning, and at noontime gave me only a crust of stale bread. She gave Grand-mère a piece that was larger.

Midafternoon, when there was a knock on the door, Maman took my lace from me. She bobbed her head to the gentleman who stood on the threshold. He was a very minor courtier; as Isabelle of the palace I would not have even noticed him. He would have been like the wallpaper. He would have noticed me instead. If I were standing beside Thérèse, he would have bowed low. Now he looked down his nose haughtily while Maman made excuses–a sick daughter as well as a sick *belle-mère*–yet she was working hard, look, here was her progress–certainly his full order done by tomorrow or the next day. He harrumphed, but he couldn't find fault with the lace, because it was perfect. I had done well.

"What a toad," I said when he was gone. "Must we work so hard for a nobody like him? He didn't even look at me. He wasn't nice to you."

"A toad!" Maman said. "A nobody! And who, pray tell, are you? You are less than no one, for all your airs, and that man has been put above you by God. And I, I would like to be able to buy some bread today. How about you?"

Maman's tirade stopped my tongue, but it made me think as well. Always before I would have thought as Maman did. The king was ordained by God, and the nobles were born into high place because God willed it. Peasants were poor because they were meant to be poor.

But how could I be a nobody one moment, and a person of rank the next? How could I, unchanged, take on both roles? Which part did God wish me to have?

Later, when we had stopped working because we could no longer see our needles in the twilight, Maman told me that she had come back from visiting me at the palace to find Grand-mère on the floor, unable to rise. She had helped Grand-mère to bed. "But she is not the same," Maman said. "I brought in the doctor. He said in these cases one never knows." She sighed. "Then he charged me ten sous."

"Why didn't you come get me?" It worried me to think of her coping alone, with George and me both away.

"You came home as soon as you could, didn't you?" I nodded. "Well, then," Maman said. "Besides, I told you, I'm never setting foot in that palace again. Nor are you, from the look of things. I can't spare you, Isabelle. Not even to curry favor with the queen."

I really wasn't well yet. After I spent a few hours concentrating on lace, my head would ache so badly I couldn't see. Tears would pour down my cheeks and my hands would begin to shake. Then Maman would bring me a cool rag and lay it across my eyes and I would sleep for a little while, and when I woke the headache would have receded enough for me to go on. At night I slept soundly. No rats.

We had too many orders, and at the same time, not enough. Too many for me to do, working alone; not enough to feed us and pay all our bills. The baker refused to extend our credit. Our landlord wanted his rent. We had most of it, but not all. He shook his fist at Maman. Meanwhile, Grand-mère stayed silent. Whenever I walked past her, she scowled without looking at me, and aimed a kick at me. I grew to expect it, and learned to jump out of her way. In a way it was comforting–it proved that part of Grand-mère was still the same.

Maman tried and tried to make lace. Her crippled fingers simply would not bend. She could no longer hold a thread tight between two fingers, nor a needle. Instead she took upon herself all the chores I had done. She haggled with the shopkeepers, she fetched our bread, she emptied our slops and cleaned the room. Walking hurt her. It was painful to watch her do my work, more painful than I could have guessed.

"Never mind," she said, when I looked up and saw her struggling with a heavy tea kettle. "You can either make the lace or do the work. You can't do both. I can only do the work, so there you are."

I longed for Thérèse and for Ernestine. I couldn't think why I never heard from them. Weren't they worried about me? Didn't they wonder why I stayed away? They could have sent word. The coachman who had driven me home knew where I lived.

Then one day when I woke from a nap, Maman was standing over me, holding a scrap of paper in her hand. "Someone delivered this for you," she said.

"Who?" My heart beat fast with hope.

"How should I know? Some dirty child."

"Was it Ernestine?"

"Not unless they're naming boys Ernestine."

"Were they from the palace? Do they want me there?"

Maman looked annoyed. "How am I to know these things? A boy knocked, handed me that piece of paper. I told him I didn't have a spare coin to give him, and he stuck his tongue out at me and ran away. That's all."

There was writing on the paper, but I couldn't make anything out of it. I'd never learned to read, and neither had Maman. The paper was fine, thick and creamy, and the letters looked well made. "It must be from Thérèse," I said. I could not think of anyone else who might write to me. "She must want me to go to her." Perhaps, I thought, she wanted me to accompany her to Saint-Cloud for the summer. I had a brief, heavenly vision of a summer spent in her company, at some lovely, calm, fresh-smelling palace, full of ponies and gardens and fun. I would be clean and wear a fresh gown every day, and eat meat off china plates.

"And if you go," Maman said. "What then?" She held my gaze in hers. She was not angry, or sad, or anything but steady. I knew what she meant, and I bowed my head. I could spend my days, and perhaps even my nights, with Thérèse. And while I did, my mother and grandmother would starve.

"If I could get the queen to buy some lace . . ." *I could go there,*

I thought, *and plead my case with Thérèse. She might understand.*

"What lace would that be?" Maman said. "We are selling all the lace you make. The problem is that you aren't making enough."

I knew Maman was not complaining. I made as much lace as I could; I worked from dawn until dusk. It was just that that was not enough. One lacemaker could not support a family.

If I had been working all along, if I had not fallen off Jacques and hurt my head, if I'd never gone to the palace in the first place, we would not be in such a bad position. We might have had a few more coins put by, to pay the doctor bills, and we wouldn't be so far behind. If I had not been so long at the palace, we would still have enough to eat.

So I knew I could not leave, no matter how much I wanted to. I put the little note carefully on the mantel. Later, when I had a chance to run some errands, I would take it and see if I could find someone who could read it to me. But a few days later the paper was gone.

"The fire was almost out," Maman said, when she saw me looking for it, "so I used the paper to rekindle it. At least that way it wasn't a total waste."

I did not bother explaining that I treasured the paper. If it was burnt, there was no getting it back. I kept the king's little box hidden in my pocket, or under my mattress, so that I wouldn't hear talk of selling it. Already Maman spoke of pawning our mirror.

If only George would come home, I thought. George could save us. He always had. And one day, at the start of summer, he did.

Chapter Ten

George!" I cried, flinging myself up from my stool. The sudden movement made my headache flare. I threw my arms around him anyhow. "Where have you been?"

He laughed and swung me around. "Paris, of course," he said. "Where else?"

"I was beginning to think the marquis went to America again," I teased him, "you were gone so long."

George's face was serious. "The marquis won't go back to America," he said. "Not now, anyhow–not when he's needed in France. And I–if I go, I'll take you with me."

I squirmed. I'd expected him to joke with me. "Grand-mère's different," I said. "She can't speak. Maman's hands are very bad. I'm making the lace. We need money. How much do you have?"

George straightened. He looked over at Grand-mère, who didn't return his gaze. She sat as she always did, twisting and tangling a tattered piece of thread in her hands. "Huh," he said. "When was this?"

"When you left," I said. "I came back, everything was a mess. My head still hurts too."

"Where's Maman?"

"Arguing with the tavern owner." We owed him for a week's worth of dinners.

George ran his fingers through his hair. "Nobody's buying lace?"

"They're buying it," I said. "They're just not paying for it, that's the problem." Courtiers were often late paying their bills. There was nothing we could do about it. "Also, I can't make enough–not enough to keep all three of us." I had never realized how much work Grand-mère did, until she no longer did it.

George put his hand into his pocket and pulled out a handful of coins. "This is all I have until the next quarter," he said. "Unless we go to Paris again–sometimes I can pick up a little extra there. How much to pay the rent?"

I told him what we still needed. "And enough to pay the tavern owner, and the baker," I said. "And to buy more thread." George divided his coins into piles. There wasn't enough.

"We'll pay the tavern half what we owe, and the baker half, and then we'll still have enough for the thread," I said, rearranging the piles. "The woman who spins thread won't give credit at all." She couldn't afford to, I knew.

"That's not all, either," I said. "We're out of laudanum, and Maman can't sleep for the pain."

George winced. Laudanum was expensive. "And you're–"

"I'm working every moment I can," I said. "It's lucky the days are long this time of year. But we can't get caught up–we're falling behind. I'm doing my best."

George sighed. "I know you are." He eyed Grand-mère. I wondered if he was thinking what I sometimes thought, that I'd never expected her to be incapable of working but still plenty capable of eating. Maman, too, I supposed, but I never begrudged Maman her food. "I'll find a way to get some money," George said. "At least enough for a little laudanum, and some bread. You turn that thread into lace quickly, will you? And tell me who owes you, and I'll see if I can't shake some coins out of them."

"I will," I said. "But what are you going to do?" If he could earn more at his job, he would have done so, long ago.

He ran his hand over his face. "I don't know. Maybe the marquis's horses don't need to eat so much. They're great fat, muscled beasts, anyhow."

I knew that George meant he would sell off some of the horses' grain. "That's stealing," I said.

"It is," he said. "It's stealing from the marquis, who is honest and has never done me any harm."

"As rich as he is, I'm sure people steal from him all the time," I said.

"Perhaps. But I never have. I've been proud of that, Bella, proud of being an honest man."

"If I'd been thinking," I said, "I would have brought home something from the palace. One of my dresses, or even a silver spoon or two." Just one of Thérèse's spoons, and we would be out of trouble.

I could go back and get one, I thought. *She would never miss it.*

George must have read my thoughts, because he came up and squeezed my shoulder. "Bad enough that I skim off a little grain. I won't have my little sister turning thief, too. And if you were caught with palace silver, it would be a hanging offense."

I knew stealing was a sin. I knew I could be hanged for it. But was it really stealing when Thérèse had so much and my mother was so thin? "Well, when I get a moment free, I'll go ask Thérèse for help. She's my friend."

George frowned. "I wouldn't count on that."

"Why ever not? Now that you're here, we can at least get that skinflint baker to let us have a little more bread. I can spare an hour to go to Thérèse."

"I wouldn't get your hopes up," George said drily. "She may have acted like your friend when it suited her, but I don't exactly see her rushing over here to lend a hand."

"She would if she knew–"

"Why should she, Bella? It would be easier for her to just hire another friend. Another child like that little Ernestine, whose parents don't make a fuss or expect any payment except that their daughter be fed."

"Ernestine's not hired," I said. "Her parents are nobles–" But I stopped. I didn't know anything about Ernestine's family.

"Her father is a bailiff," George said. "The head groom knows him. Her mother was a chambermaid. The queen arranged for her to be Madame Royale's companion because she was the right age, and a girl, and because her family wouldn't fuss over anything."

"All that may be true," I said, "but it doesn't mean Thérèse isn't Ernestine's true friend."

"I don't think she worries whether Ernestine's family is fed," George said. "I don't think she'll worry about yours, either. I'm not trying to speak badly of her. She's a princess. Royals aren't like regular people. I doubt she has true feelings for you or anyone else. I saw myself how she treated you like a trained puppy, to come whenever she whistled and do whatever she pleased."

I looked up, stung. "She did not! What a stupid thing to say!"

"I spent enough time visiting you," he replied. "I kept my eyes open. They dressed you up and let you pretend to be someone you're not, and if it suited Thérèse to spend time with you, she did. If it didn't, she went where she liked and left you alone."

"I was tired," I said.

"It was no good, Bella. Admit that the queen hired you to play with her daughter–only notice that she didn't even pay you for your work."

Certainly Thérèse ordered me about. She had a right to: She was a princess, after all. But she was also kind, and so was everyone at the palace. I thought of the daily doctor visits, the fresh nightgowns, the soup they spooned into me when I could not sit up to eat. The king's box, which I kept beneath my mattress.

I thought of Thérèse huddling against me when the rats were bad.

"George," I said quietly. "Thérèse and Ernestine love me. They do."

George looked ready to make a retort, but Maman came in just then, exclaiming with joy when she saw him. She began to recite to him the list of our woes; he cut her off, and with a kiss to her cheek swept his coins into his pocket, and went to battle with the landlord.

Maman eased herself into her chair. "Well, I hope we'll eat something besides bread tonight. Isabelle! Why aren't you working? George will help, but he can't do enough on his own."

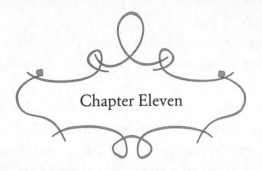

Chapter Eleven

A few days later George came to check on us. He brought a pail of the pork stew the stable hands had been given for dinner. Grand-mère, the greedy pig, grabbed it from him and began shoveling great fingerfuls of it into her mouth. George wrestled it from her and poured a portion into her bowl. I carefully anchored my thread and set my lace aside before eating mine.

"Maman's at the baker's," I said. The stew was wonderful, greasy and salty and still warm. Even with George's money we were eating almost nothing except bread, and the cost of bread was staggering since last year's crops had fared badly. Soon there would be another wheat harvest and the price might fall. I hoped so.

I was grateful for the stew but still angry with George, and I didn't talk to or look at him while I ate. I thought he'd leave, but he stayed, watching me, and eventually he asked, "Do you know why the marquis went to America to fight?"

That had been when I was a tiny baby, but Maman had told me about it. "Because America was fighting England, and France hates England."

"Not really," he said. "France hates England, true, and that may have been why the king and queen supported the

Americans. The marquis fought because Americans believe that all men are created equal. They didn't want to be ruled by the British king, or by any king. They believe in liberty, in equality. So does the marquis. The Americans think that people should govern themselves. The marquis thinks that too."

I had seen the Marquis de Lafayette from a distance, walking though the palace with the king. He was bald-headed but extraordinarily grand; he looked more royal than the king. He may have believed in equality; he still acted like nobility.

"Of course people cannot govern themselves," I said. "Who would tell them what to do?"

"They decide what to do," he said. "They vote. Not only the rich people. Anyone who owns land."

I snorted. "How ridiculous. Even peasants own land. Our king was ordained by God. He rules because it is God's will that he do so."

"If that were true," my brother said, "wouldn't God make him do a better job?"

I froze. My mouth dropped open. That thought was treason. George knew it too. He looked nearly as shocked as I felt. "You shouldn't–," I whispered.

"I know, I know," he said, waving his hand. "I'm careful, I promise. But think about it, Bella. For all our troubles, we–you and I–are wealthy. We worry about going hungry, but really, when have we ever done it? When have we ever not had a fire in winter? Half our country goes without bread while the king and queen frolic at Versailles. A good king, a wise king, would see this, and change it. Our king sees nothing, and does less."

I wished George wouldn't exaggerate so. How could people be hungry? It was summer, a growing season. Surely it could not be a tough time for so many.

George found some old tack at the stable that he said no one wanted anymore, and sold it. He upped his horses' grain ration, then sold the extra. One of the courtiers had a lucky run at the card table, and when I went to him with our bill, for the tenth time, his pockets were full of money and he paid me in coin. So we did better for a little while. Maman had laudanum, and could sleep again. We ate mutton stew three times a week. We paid a month's rent, and had enough bread.

I didn't hear from Thérèse. Maman forbade me to go near the palace. "It didn't help us before," she said. "I thought it might, but I was wrong."

More weeks passed. I barely stepped out of doors; my whole world compressed itself to strips of linen, yards of white thread. Was this how Maman and Grand-mère had felt for all these years? I hated lace. My time at the palace seemed like a half-remembered dream.

Had Thérèse forgotten me?

Grand-mère liked to hog the best seat by the window, in full light. Maman and I didn't think she realized she wasn't working. She sat at the window twisting the same piece of thread, and she mumbled to herself. She ate when we put food in front of her, and when it grew dark she went to bed. I worked at the other window seat, with my lace and linen ground cloth spread on the shelf built beneath the window. The sun didn't reach that window quite as well, but as Maman said, I didn't need so much light for my young eyes. Also, in summer the sun shone so bright.

We were sitting side by side one morning when Grand-mère looked up and gave a snort. She still didn't speak, but she bumped me with her elbow and pointed outside.

One of the queen's carriages had stopped at the corner.

The royal carriages never went through the town. There was never any need for them to do so–the road to Paris ran straight out the front gate of the palace. *Thérèse,* I thought. My heart gave a sudden leap. I threw my work down and ran for the door.

I met Ernestine coming up the stairs. "Clochette!" she cried. She hugged me, and I hugged her. "Are you well?" she asked anxiously.

My skirt and shift were old, and my vest was partially unlaced. I knew my hair wasn't combed. My hands were clean, so I wouldn't soil the lace, but the rest of me not so much. "I'm fine," I said, "just not dressed for the palace. Come up."

When I went through the door, I thought how our squalid room must look to someone from the palace. I was glad for a moment that it was Ernestine, who after all went home to her own family every night and whose father was only a bailiff, and not Thérèse. Then I was ashamed of my gladness. Maman and I did our best, and surely Thérèse loved me no matter where I lived. At least Maman had emptied the chamber pots before she went out to buy bread.

Grand-mère looked at Ernestine. For a moment a light blazed up in her eyes. She had not spoken once in a month, but now she said, quite clearly and disgustedly, "Austrichienne."

It was an unfortunate word. Really it meant "A woman who comes from Austria." The problem was that it also combined the words, "austrich," or "ostrich," and "chienne," or "female dog." Most French people disliked Austrians, and they liked the fact that "Austrichienne" also meant "ostrich-dog."

It was an evil way to speak of the queen.

"Pay no attention," I told Ernestine. "She's my father's mother. She's lost her mind."

Grand-mère spat on the floor. Ernestine grinned. I'd forgotten how her eyes could sparkle. "Who does she think I am?" she asked me.

"Grand-mère," I said loudly. "This is my friend Ernestine. This isn't the queen or her daughter."

Grand-mère turned away, muttering to herself.

"We've been worried," Ernestine said. "Thérèse and I. You haven't come back once, or sent word, or replied to our letter. One of the physicians said these head cases can be strange–said maybe you'd died or something and we never knew." She paused and took a deep breath. "If you're not dead, why haven't you come back? Why didn't you let us know?"

Once again I was glad it was Ernestine who came, not Thérèse. I explained all that had happened, and I knew that Ernestine understood where Thérèse might not have. I wiped out a mug and gave her some tea, and she drank it solemnly. Before she left, she took both my hands in her own. "Thérèse says to tell you that you must come back," she said. "We miss you. Your garden is growing without you. The riding master keeps bringing out a third pony. You must come back."

"I will," I said. "I will just as soon as I can."

She kissed my cheek and left. The bright carriage rolled away. When Maman returned with a loaf of bread and another hank of thread, she found me in bed with the covers pulled over my head, silently crying. I told her all about Ernestine's visit, and what Thérèse had said.

"She does want me," I choked. "She does."

Maman looked impassive. "Do you have that collar finished yet? Tears and promises don't buy bread."

I got up and went back to work. What choice did I have?

Chapter Twelve

The very next day a second carriage, much smaller and plainer, stopped on our corner. A woman I recognized as one of Thérèse's servants came to the door. When I opened it, she asked to see what lace I had on hand. I didn't have any extra–we worked to order, with the cost of thread so high–but I hastily pulled out the collar I had finished the night before. Maman had planned to deliver it that morning. It was for a woman's dress, a delicate pattern of leaves and flowers. The servant examined it closely, then quietly offered to pay me three livres for it.

Sixty sols. A loaf of bread cost five sols. The thread for the collar had cost ten. I'd expected to get twenty sols for the collar.

My mouth dropped. "But I made it for Madame de–"

"Yes," Maman said quickly, closing her hand over the money. "Thank you very much. Please tell your mistress we appreciate her patronage. Would she like lace cuffs to match?"

Her use of the word "patron" recalled me to my senses. "Please tell her thank you," I said. "Please send her my kind regards."

It would help us, yes. It would be the sort of thing that Grand-mère and Maman had hoped for when they'd first sent me to the palace. It could be the saving of us.

But oh, horrors! It would be me, only me, making the lace. By myself. No one to help me.

The servant leaned forward and said quietly, "Madame Royale desires that you should dine with her tomorrow."

All the words I'd learned at court came easily back to my tongue. "Please to tell Madame Royale that I shall be humbly glad to do so." The woman bowed and went away, and I watched with a pounding heart as the carriage bowled down the street.

"Better get busy on another collar," Maman said, as though she had not overheard the invitation. Not an invitation, I corrected myself. A royal summons.

"Must I?" I wanted to bathe, and wash my hair. Thérèse would be appalled by my filth.

"You just sold Madame de Saint-Auguste's lace to someone else," Maman said. "You need something to give Madame de Saint-Auguste."

"But Thérèse–"

"Has bought one collar only," Maman said. "It's a help, yes, and she paid more than she should, which is a good sign. But not so good that we can lose all our other customers. Get busy."

I got busy. By superhuman effort I managed to finish the new collar by noon the next day. I flung it down on the table, finished, for Maman to press and deliver. I didn't have time for a bath, but I washed my face and hands, tidied my hair, and put on my too-tight dress. Then I ran full tilt to the palace.

I felt like I had come home. The crowds, the stench, the gilt and glory, the dog racing down the corridor with a jeweled shoe in its mouth, all seemed perfectly familiar. I pounded on the door to Thérèse's rooms, and the maidservant bowed to me when she opened it.

Thérèse was standing with her back to me at the far side of the room. She turned and looked at me, and something in her cool expression froze my smile. I rushed toward her. She looked me up and down.

"Aren't you glad to see me?" I said.

"You should have come back earlier," she said. "You said you would keep me safe from the rats."

"I wanted to," I said. "Grand-mère had a stroke and Maman is ill–"

"But I needed you."

"So did they."

Thérèse's nose crinkled. "You *said* you were my true friend."

"I am your true friend." Anger blazed up in me. "Yet what would you have had me do? Come shield you from nightmares, you who are surrounded by governesses and have more food than you can eat, while my mother and grandmother were turned out hungry into the street?"

She drew herself up taller as only Thérèse could. "And if they were going to be put out, you could save them? A girl like you? You could keep them housed and fed?"

"I could and I did," I spat back. "I had no choice." I knew that wasn't entirely true. As hard and as skillfully as I had worked, I hadn't been able to do enough. I'd needed George to steal for us. Thérèse looked shocked, and I knew I should back down, but fury kept me going. "I am not like you," I said. "I am not royal nor noble nor gentry. I must work or my family starves. I am not ashamed that I did not come to you. I would be ashamed if I had. I would be ashamed if I were you, standing here judging me when you know nothing about how real people live. *Nothing*."

I turned on my heel and marched back toward the door. Tears

of hot fury coursed down my face. The servants moved aside, looking horrified. I had nearly reached the door when Thérèse said, in a softer voice, "Wait."

I almost didn't stop. Part of me wanted to stomp out of the palace and never return. But the part of me that was still Clochette came to a halt. I heard Thérèse's measured steps behind me.

"Turn around," she said. "Oh, Clochette. You're crying. Here." She handed me her handkerchief–lace-trimmed–and I swiped at my tears.

"Of course I know you would not lie to me," she said. "I should not have said what I did. You are right, there are many things about common people that I do not know. I do not need to know them. But you are wrong to say that I judge you, Clochette. I do not. Will you please come with me to eat?"

Slowly I nodded. That was as close to an apology as I was ever going to get from her.

"You should curtsy," she said. "You should curtsy to me when you first come into my presence."

The servants curtsied, of course, but Ernestine and I never did. I looked at Thérèse. She waited. I curtsied. She nodded. "Come," she said, "I have your dress waiting for you, and hot water for your face, and perfume for your hair."

She showed me the dress, and the new slippers that had been made to fit my feet. She had one of the servants comb my hair.

We sat down to dinner, Thérèse, Ernestine, Madame de Polignac, and I, just as we used to, but everything felt different to me. "After dinner we have a riding lesson," Thérèse said. "Your new pony is very much calmer. Father promises. Are you afraid?"

I swallowed my mouthful of veal and patted my lips with a

linen napkin. I remembered my last terrifying ride, and how my head had hurt for so long. "Afraid of a pony?" I said. "Of course not, Thérèse. Nothing frightens me." Except hunger, and Grand-mère, and not making enough lace.

She smiled a little, the first smile she'd given me.

"Madame de Polignac," I said, while the meats were being cleared away and little cakes set out, "to be honored with the position of Thérèse's governess, you must be a very great friend of the queen."

Madame de Polignac smiled. "But of course," she said. "We have been intimates for years."

"And yet you must not hold this position without pay," I persisted. "You must be compensated for your loyal service."

Madame de Polignac and Thérèse looked astonished. Ernestine took a quick sip of wine to hide her smile. "Her Majesty amply repays my loyalty," Madame de Polignac said.

"Just so," I said. "You are part of her court, and you hold a high position. You must be rewarded. Thérèse, Ernestine and I are your court. You do not pay us for our friendship, which is yours without question, but of course out of your generosity you wish to reward us for our dedication. Ernestine takes her meals here and receives her education. I do not ask for anything so fine. I wish for only a fraction of that, for only twenty livres a week, so that I may care for my crippled mother and feeble grandmother."

After paying for thread, I might earn five livres a week making lace for the gentry. If I was lucky. But we needed more than that to survive.

Thérèse's chin went up. "But I desire that you dine with me," she said. "I desire that you eat this meal with me, every day."

She smiled down the table at Ernestine. "Ernestine here never complains of her lot. Not like you. She doesn't speak to me of family, of obligation, of money."

"She has a father–"

"Nor will I pay you for coming here," Thérèse interrupted. "I command that you spend your afternoons with me, and as my true friend you shall not say no. But I will make you my official lacemaker. You, and you alone. You will bring me the lace you make, and my servants will pay you twenty livres. Madame de Polignac will give you something now, and the rest you will get on quarter-days. That is how it will be."

It was not a question, so it did not require an answer, but I nodded. I wondered if Thérèse had any idea how much I hated making lace. I wondered if she had any idea how grateful I was, how relieved.

"No more collars," she added. "It was a fine collar, but I don't wear collars. I want yards of lace, two inches wide, to trim my petticoats and nightgowns."

"It will be beautiful," I said. "I promise you will be satisfied." I leaned forward. "And now, tell me about this new pony. I assure you, I don't wish to fall off again."

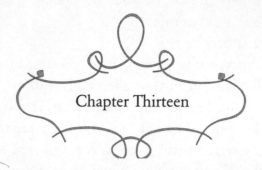

Chapter Thirteen

Neither Thérèse nor Ernestine spoke of my lacemaking. From that day on, I woke at first light. I ate a roll and drank some milk. I made lace until the church bells chimed noon. Then I climbed off my stool and hurried away to dine with Thérèse. By the time I reached the palace she and Ernestine would be finished with their lessons. I would eat with them, and we would play for the entire afternoon.

I was careful to always eat heartily at the palace, so that when I returned home, I needed no more than a scrap of bread. Madame de Polignac had given me enough money to buy thread, and to last until the quarter-day if we stayed frugal.

"Lacemaker to the Princess Royale," Maman said approvingly. "It sounds well." Now that she was not so worried, Maman slept better and was not as cross. A little plumpness had returned to her cheeks too, and her hands were not so swollen.

When I ripped the skirt of one of my court dresses trying to climb a tree near the statue of Venus–Thérèse had dared me to–ripped it right in front, where it would be impossible to mend, Madame de Polignac smiled gently and brushed away my tears. "Children should climb trees," she said. "It's no matter, dear. It's only a dress."

It was only a dress. Silk taffeta. I had a dozen, at least. The queen had hundreds.

Maman had two dresses, neither silk. Grand-mère had only one, and had to go to bed in her shift on wash days.

When it rained, we spent the hours indoors. Thérèse taught me embroidery. I was quick to learn, which was hardly a surprise. But when I suggested I might teach her and Ernestine to make lace, they both looked offended. "Lace is made by tradespeople," Thérèse said. "It's like fabric. It's something you buy."

"I'm a tradesperson," I said. "I make lace."

"Not here you don't," Thérèse said. Her smugness infuriated me.

"At home I do," I said. "As did my mother and my grandmother before me."

"At home you are a lacemaker," Thérèse said. "Here you are my true friend, Clochette."

"I am glad to be Clochette," I said. "You know that. But I am not one person here and another at home. I am one person only."

"You are two people," Thérèse said. "But when I grow up, you will be only one. I will hold court the way the queen my mother does. You and Ernestine will be my ladies-in-waiting. We will all dress in jewels, and dance, and play cards, and stay up past midnight the way the court does. We will be beautiful. You will live with me, and you will never make lace again."

I could allow myself to hope. It wasn't completely impossible. Half the nobles were Nobles of the Sword, raised to nobility through service to the king and queen.

"Of course," Thérèse said thoughtfully, "it will be in some other country. I wish I knew which one."

"But France, of course," I said. "Why should you have to leave?"

Thérèse laughed out loud. "France! Who would I marry in France?"

I opened my mouth and then shut it. I had never thought about it before. Thérèse, a king's daughter, could not marry beneath her.

"Perhaps my cousin the crown prince of Naples," Thérèse said. "Of course, I suppose I could marry one of my cousins here, but I hate them and would rather not."

"The church wouldn't allow it," Ernestine said. "Marrying your cousin!"

"Of course they would," Thérèse said, "for royalty. The only good thing about marrying the wretched Duke of Angoulême would be that I could stay in France then."

"It's years before you need to worry," I said. Most women worked for ten years or more to get a dowry. Maman married at twenty-seven, and Grand-mère had been older than that. Not that Thérèse would need to work.

Thérèse shrugged. "My mother came from Austria to marry my father when she was fourteen. They were betrothed before that, and I imagine the negotiations took a while. I'm almost ten now. It won't be long."

Ernestine and I looked at each other. Being ladies-in-waiting here at Versailles was one thing; being ladies-in-waiting in some heathen unfamiliar place, Naples or Spain or Hungary, was quite another.

"Did your mother even speak French when she came here?" I asked.

Thérèse shrugged. "She does now."

Ernestine spoke in a low voice. "Does she ever go home?"

Now Thérèse looked irritated. "She is home," she said. "She has a different home. And that is what will happen to me, and you will come with me, because I will want you. You must promise me. Promise you will be my ladies, wherever I go."

I thought with a sudden pang of George and Maman. Becoming Thérèse's lady would be very agreeable, but how could I go to Naples and leave them behind?

"My family–," I began.

"Grows tiresome," said Thérèse. "I won't see my mother again either, you know. Nor my brothers, nor my father, nor Madame de Polignac."

"I promise," Ernestine said. "I will come with you wherever you go."

"Clochette," Thérèse said sternly. I looked at her. She looked back, glowering, and then suddenly her eyes softened and she smiled. "You don't like to give in, I know, but you are my true friend and you must stay with me."

"I will," I said at last. "I will stay with you, and keep you safe from rats forever."

"Wherever I go," she said.

"Wherever."

"Whenever I go."

"Whenever."

Thérèse laughed with joy. "I know you keep your promises. We will never be parted."

The queen sailed in a few minutes later to visit us. She pulled Thérèse onto her lap and kissed and hugged her. Thérèse held herself stiff. I leaned sideways just a bit, until my shoulder touched the queen's shoulder. She smelled so heavenly, much better than most of the people at Versailles. She admired our work, she praised our industry, and she sailed out again.

"Why aren't you nicer to her?" I asked Thérèse.

Thérèse sniffed. "She's not that nice to me."

"She kisses you, she hugs you," I said. "My mother doesn't. I wish she did."

Thérèse looked bitter. "She barely glanced at my embroidery. She asks questions, but never listens to the answers. Whenever we walk to the chapel to hear Mass, she always walks ahead. She never looks back to see if I'm with her. The king my father walks with me. He takes me by the hand."

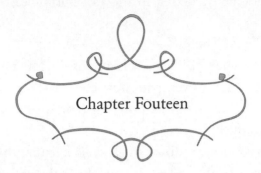

Chapter Fouteen

Ernestine's mother died. The queen herself brought us the news. She held Ernestine close and wiped her tears, while Thérèse and I held each other and wept as well.

Ernestine's mother had been ill with consumption the entire time I'd known Ernestine, but she had grown much worse while I had been gone. Thérèse had warned me, and she and I had been as gentle with Ernestine as we could.

"Maman." A high little voice broke into our sobs. "Maman! Why are they crying? Clochette and Ernestine and my sister?"

It was Charles, Thérèse's little brother, the Duke of Normandy. After his nap he often escaped from his nursemaids and spent part of the afternoon with us.

The queen made room for him on her knee. "They are crying because they are sad," she said.

"Oh." He put his finger into his mouth and sucked it. "Will they stop?"

"Yes," said the queen. "But not for a while. They will be sad, and you must be kind to them. Ernestine, dear"–she stroked Ernestine's face–"I've sent for a carriage to take you home."

Ernestine nodded. Tears rolled down her face, and she breathed with great shuddering gasps. "I'll go too," I said quickly, thinking of poor Ernestine by herself in the vast bumpy carriage. "I'll go with her."

"Me too," said Thérèse.

"Very well." The queen gave a last consoling hug to Ernestine. "When the funeral is over, you must come back to Versailles for good. You must live with us now. I'll send a servant with you, to tell your father."

The carriage rolled down the wide avenues of the park. "Where do you live?" I asked. I knew the bailiff must live on the grounds, but I'd never asked where.

"The other side of the woods," Ernestine said. Her voice was still muffled by tears. "My father and my grandparents share a cottage."

We trundled through the woods to a part of the parkland I'd never visited before, and at last stopped in front of a tiny, dilapidated cottage. The cottage shocked me. I remembered how I had felt embarrassed when Ernestine came to the two rooms Maman and Grand-mère and I shared. Now I saw that we were wealthy by comparison. We had glass in our windows; we had wood in our fireplace; we had linen curtains and mats on the floor and furniture. Ernestine's family's cottage, huddled on the edge of the damp, cold woods, had oiled leather covering the open windows. When her father opened the door and rushed to meet us, I could see dirt floors, a smoky fire. Everything smelled decayed. The other children in the yard were barefoot and grubby. When they ran forward crying, "Marie, Marie," I didn't know who they meant. I had forgotten that Ernestine was not really named Ernestine.

When Thérèse and I were on our way home, I whispered, "I didn't know Ernestine was so poor."

Thérèse looked puzzled. "She's not. Her father has a job. Plus, she stays with me."

"But the family–the little children–and that cottage–" I didn't know how to say it. "It must be damp there, and cold in the winter."

"Sometimes my mother sends blankets. My mother is very generous."

"But if Ernestine's mother–" I swallowed hard. "If she'd lived somewhere better, maybe she wouldn't have gotten consumption. Maybe she wouldn't have died."

Thérèse gave me a long solemn look. I couldn't tell what she was thinking. She said to the servant in the coach with us, "Stop the coach." The servant bawled out the window to the driver. "I want to go to the Petit Trianon," she told him. "We are going to visit my brother."

After Ernestine had told me that the Dauphin, Louis Joseph, was ill, I was careful not to mention him to Thérèse. Only once had I commented that we never saw him. "I see him often," Thérèse had said, lapsing into sudden reserve. "I see him often when you're not here."

"The Dauphin my brother must have special tutors," she'd added. "He must learn to be king."

"Does he study with your cousins?" I remembered the rough boys I'd met on my first day at the palace.

Thérèse pursed her lips. "Of course not."

I had learned that the queen despised the king's two younger brothers and their wives, and their children. "My mother was married for many years before I was born," Thérèse explained. "My uncles and aunts laughed at her. And if the king died without children, then my cousins would inherit the throne."

"They can't now," I had said, and she had smiled.

Besides the huge main palace, there were two smaller palaces on the grounds of Versailles, the Trianon and the Petit Trianon. They were the personal property of the king and queen; the court could not go there without invitation. I had seen them from the outside only. The gardens around them were beautiful.

Our carriage stopped outside the Petit Trianon. Thérèse went up the steps and swept inside. "We have come to see my brother," she told a startled footman. "Is he still here?"

The footman bowed low. "Yes, Madame."

Thérèse led the way through a warren of rooms, all strung together like the grand rooms at Versailles, but smaller; equally beautiful but more delicate. The walls didn't remind me of beefsteak here. Most of them were painted a soft white, with beautiful plaster moldings of flowers and leaves.

Everything, every tiny detail, was luxurious. Here the air even smelled fresh and clean. How could Thérèse not see the contrast between her life and Ernestine's?

"My mother brings my brother here whenever he feels especially bad," Thérèse said. She opened one last door, and we went into a bedchamber. A tiny, frail boy half-rose from the bed. He smiled. "Sister!" he said.

There were a few servants in the corner of the room, but nobody important; the prince was quite alone. His bed had been set beneath a low window. An open book lay beside him.

Thérèse went up to him. "Have you been reading?"

"No. Just resting." He coughed, raising his thin hand to cover his mouth. "Who have you brought?"

"This is Clochette. I told you about her."

The boy looked at me frankly. I tried not to stare at him. His fair hair was pushed straight back from his thin face. His eyes looked terribly large, and his lips were as pale as milk. When he turned away from us to cough again, I could see that his back, beneath his linen shift, was twisted, hunched and lumpy, deformed. His legs were so thin I wondered if he could stand.

"Are you cold?" Thérèse asked. She twitched a silk comforter over his sticklike legs.

"Not very." He coughed again, three times in less than a minute. This time he put a handkerchief to his mouth, and when he pulled it away, I saw that it was dotted with blood. "Thérèse said you make lace," he told me.

"Yes, monsieur. When I'm not at the palace."

"She said you were becoming good at riding horses and milking cows, but you still weren't much of a gardener."

"Yes, monsieur." For all his frailty he looked more regal than his father. "Thérèse has a gray pony that she lets me ride. I like it very much." The pony, a replacement for bad Jacques, was named Mercredi. I loved him.

"That's good. Perhaps someday you and Thérèse will go hunting together." He coughed, but it turned into a yawn. His eyelids fluttered.

Thérèse immediately stood. "I'll come back tomorrow if you're still here," she said. He waved a thin hand at us, and we went away.

Back inside the coach I didn't know what to say. I knew now that the rumors must be true; the Dauphin was dying. I understood why the king and queen kept him out of sight.

"How old is he?" I asked.

"Nearly seven," Thérèse said. She looked angry and bitter.

"He has consumption. Just like Ernestine's mother. It is not caused by poverty or dampness. If it were, he would be well."

I nodded.

"It is God's will," whispered Thérèse. She closed her eyes and leaned her head against the cushions in the carriage.

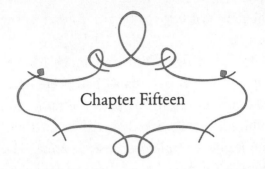

Chapter Fifteen

Ernestine came back to the palace after a few days. She was given a bed in Thérèse's bedroom, and a maid of her own, and any number of new nightgowns and cloaks and pelisses, but she remained sad and subdued. Thérèse and I were gentle with her. "She loved her mother," Thérèse whispered to me one day.

I nodded.

"It must be a wonderful thing," Thérèse whispered, out of earshot, "to love your mother that much."

"I love my mother that much," I said. "I would be that sad if she died."

"Hmm." Thérèse looked at me skeptically. "I think I would sadder if my brother died than if my mother did. I would be very sad if my father died. My father loves me more than my mother does."

The Duke of Normandy covered the queen with hugs and slobbery kisses; Thérèse never did. I never understood. If the queen had wanted me to, I would have hugged and kissed her myself. "She kisses us and says how much she loves us, and then she goes away to the Trianon for days without us," Thérèse said. "She says she hates the court, but she leaves me here. I don't like it."

"You said she stayed with you when you were sick," I reminded her.

"I would like to not have to be sick for her to stay with me," said Thérèse.

At home I tried to figure out how much Maman loved me. I was making a little less lace than I had been, because we were paid so well, and because I was paid the same no matter how much I produced. I still worked at it three or four hours every day, not wanting to completely cheat Thérèse. The rest of my morning, though, I did the heavy chores, fetching water and lifting the pots on and off the stove. In the afternoons, while I was gone, a girl from the tavern came up and for a sol or two did any little thing Maman and Grand-mère needed, and then in the evenings I was home. We spoke of hiring a servant–a girl my age from the country would work cheap–but Maman hesitated. She didn't trust our current prosperity.

"Thérèse will not desert me," I said one night, arguing that we should indeed hire a girl. I thought it was beneath me, a little, to empty the chamber pots. Clochette wouldn't do it, after all. No one would dream of asking her to.

"The country is in debt," Maman said. "Even the king is running out of money. What if Thérèse can't pay you anymore? What would we do then?"

"Thérèse could pay me," I said. "Twenty livres a week is nothing. It would not pay for one tenth the food eaten by Thérèse's servants alone." I'd never forgotten the vast kitchens on the ground floor.

Maman shook her head. "Such waste," she said.

I began to hear murmurings everywhere, of how much

money the war in America had cost France, of how much the government spent, of how much the king and queen wasted on extravagance, of how taxes would be raised and people left hungry. I heard the rumors, never at court, but around the town and sometimes at the stables when I visited George.

"Two yards of taffeta," George said to me one day.

"What?"

"I heard the queen uses two yards of silk taffeta every day, to cover the basket her ladies carry her gloves in."

I had seen the queen's ladies walking behind her with a basket covered in a fine green cloth. "So?"

"Two *fresh* yards, every day. New cloth, every day! Does the cloth covering the queen's gloves wear out?"

I knew the answer, though I didn't like to admit it to George. "Probably one of the ladies has the rights to the queen's taffeta. She probably keeps it and sells it."

George gave a snort of disgust. "It would take a weaver, what, an entire day of work to weave those two yards? And four women to spin a day's worth of thread for the weaver. Five people laboring a full day so that the queen's gloves may be covered! Does that seem reasonable, Bella?"

But for all the waste, no one at the court seemed to think they would run out of money, and I said so to Maman. "It can't happen," I said. "But if it did, Thérèse would still take care of us."

Maman shook her head at me. "Foolish girl. You don't understand."

Another day: "Ignorant girl."

Another: "You are not a princess, you know, for all you spend time with one."

When the queen saw me, she called me beautiful. Elegant. Smart. One of her favorite girls in the world.

I hoped my mother loved me.

Not long after Ernestine returned to the palace the queen entered Thérèse's rooms wearing a delighted smile. "Come, my lovely little maidens," she said, beckoning us to sit beside her on the low sofa by the wall. "I've brought you all a little something to cheer you." In her hands she held a small gold-covered chest. She opened it to show us three gold rings. One had a ruby, for Ernestine, one an emerald, for Thérèse, and one a diamond, for me. "My sisters and I used to have rings like this," she said gaily. "I thought you should have them too–you are almost sisters, you know."

Ernestine smiled, though I could see it cost her an effort to do so. No gift in a gilt box could staunch her sorrow. Thérèse's smile was also a little dutiful, but I made mine as big and bright as I could, and I threw my arms around Her Majesty.

"I can see that I've pleased at least one of you," she said, laughing. "Put them on, now. Let me see them on your hands." We put the rings on, each of us moving them from finger to finger until we found where they would fit. They sparkled in the sunlight.

"Beautiful," the queen said. "Beautiful jewelry, beautiful hands." She kissed each of us on our fingertips before she went away.

"She's so kind," I said. "Thérèse, how can you be so cold?"

"If she loves us so much, why doesn't she stay with us? Why does she give us gifts and then go away?"

"She's very busy," Ernestine murmured.

"Pah. She complains all the time of being bored. This ring is nice, I suppose, but it's very plain. Some of the courtiers have larger gems on the heels of their shoes."

That was not how my mother reacted to the ring. She stared at it in awed silence, as if it were alive, and deadly. "I don't know," she said at last. "You shouldn't wear it. We should put it away, for safekeeping."

"The queen will be insulted if I take it off," I said. "She said so."

"I don't know," Maman repeated. "It's too much. It's not safe."

"How can a ring be dangerous?"

"Think, Isabelle. That ring would pay our rent for a year. That ring would pay *anyone's* rent for a year."

I loved the ring, but really, I couldn't believe it would be worth that much. "It's plain," I said. "Some of the courtiers have larger gems on the heels of their shoes."

"Shame!" hissed Maman. "It's not enough that I should have a stupid girl. Now I have a disrespectful one as well!"

I clutched my hand around it. "I can't sell it," I said. "The queen would be displeased."

"Of course not, stupid! Only realize what you're wearing. Don't flaunt it around town. Someone will steal it, else. They might hurt you to get it. At the palace you might be safe. Around town–a common girl shouldn't have such a thing. Perhaps you'd better keep it at the palace."

I didn't. I did start carrying the king's little box in my pocket. On my trips to and from the palace I locked the ring inside it. At the palace, and at home, I wore my ring in plain sight. I slept with my hand atop the blankets.

Chapter Sixteen

Less than a week later, the royal family went to their summer palace, miles away, at Saint-Cloud. Ernestine went with them. I wished so much to be invited that I prayed about it, and lighted candles in the palace chapel, but Thérèse didn't ask me. I didn't know why. She would be gone a month, maybe more, and I was stuck home all day with Maman and Grand-mère.

"What did you think?" George asked me roughly. "That you were part of the royal family?" I had gone to the stables to tell him about it. I had expected more sympathy.

"No!" I stamped my foot. "I just think she might have taken me. She said before that she might, and then not a word when it was time to go." I had told her that I would miss her, and she'd nodded her head but never said she would miss me. Ernestine kissed my cheeks and looked sorry, but Thérèse did not.

"She's the princess," George told me. "You're not."

"It's not fair!"

"No," he said. His firm tone surprised me. "I quite agree."

"She shouldn't have gone without me!"

"That's not what I mean." George swept the aisle, hesitating before he spoke again. "You've gotten properly spoiled, haven't you? Life in the palace suits you?"

"Why wouldn't it suit me?" I shot back. "They care about me there, and it's lovely."

He sighed. "Bella, you're like another servant."

"I'm not," I said. "I am Thérèse's lacemaker, there's no shame in that."

George snorted. "A ten-year-old with her own lacemaker! I see some shame in that."

"Even if I was a servant, so what? You're a servant, and you don't seem to think it's so bad."

His eyes blazed, then darkened. The anger on his face gave way to a deep, terrible sadness. "I'd give anything to do something else," he said. "Something learned. To be one of those city merchants with a book under his arm and a fine curled wig. To sit in a chair all day long."

My mouth dropped open. I never knew this. "Why don't you, then?"

He laughed bitterly. "How? Where is it that I may learn to read? What should I do, walk to Paris and go up to the shop owners, and say, 'Here–hire me'?"

"Yes, do," I said. "I'm making enough for Maman now–we'll be fine without your money."

"You don't understand the world, Bella," he said. "Nobody in Paris will hire me for a job that's any better or different from what I do now. To work in a shop you must first be an apprentice. To buy an apprenticeship costs money–more money than I could save in ten years. I'm stuck here, I truly am. It's not so terrible. There are worse things than to shovel horse manure all your life."

"When Thérèse marries, you won't have to," I said. "I'm

going to be one of her ladies. I'll take care of you then. It'll only be a few years from now."

He stared at me as though I'd suddenly grown another head, then laughed hard and long.

"It's true," I said. I kicked him to make him stop laughing. "We've promised each other. I'm going to go with her, wherever she goes when she marries. I'll wear beautiful gowns and she'll find me a wonderful husband, and I'll be real nobility, just like Madame de Polignac."

"You won't become noble," George said. At last he stopped laughing. "That's ridiculous. Please understand how ridiculous it is. This is why I don't like your going so much to the palace. You're still a child. You begin to believe these silly dreams, and one day they're going to break your heart."

I reached into my pocket for my ring. "Look," I said. "The queen herself–"

George waved it away. "Maman told me. It's wrong, Bella. You're not going to grow up to wear silk dresses like a princess–"

"I wear silk dresses now," I said. "At the palace, I dress the same as Thérèse."

"It doesn't make you Thérèse," George said. "That whole palace–that whole world–it's nothing but a sham. Empty people spending money they don't have on, foolishness and vanity."

"Why do you care?" I asked him. "If your life is the same no matter what they do, why do you care?"

"You don't see what I see," George said. "In Paris, or on the road there and back. People are suffering. They are angry. The king and the court ignore them."

"If people are suffering," I said, "it's not Thérèse's fault. If it weren't for her kindness, I would be shut up all day, trying to make enough lace to keep us in bread, and failing, too! Thérèse–the queen–they are helping. Helping. Not hurting."

"Helping you," George said. "Ignoring all of France."

I didn't know whether he was right about people suffering or not, but I did know I wasn't going to listen to him prosing anymore. "When they help me, they help you," I said. "Or are you still stealing horse feed from the marquis?" I turned on my heel and went out.

Rather than go home I turned my steps toward the palace. It was echoing and empty. The courtiers had gone back to their own estates; even most of the servants were below-stairs. I wandered through Thérèse's bare glittering rooms, setting cushions to right on chairs, and picking up a toy horse that the Duke of Normandy must have dropped. A chambermaid came in and gave me a brief smile. She gathered some old linens out of a press, and left without looking back.

The hallways, usually so crushed with people, were empty and swept clean. Breezes ruffled the curtains, and the air smelled so much sweeter than normal. Turning the corner, I saw again the candle boy I'd met on my very first day at Versailles.

It was odd, but I recognized him immediately, though we hadn't spoken once in the intervening months. "Hello!" I said. "You're Pierre, aren't you?"

He stared at me suspiciously. "Who says?"

"I'm Isabelle," I said. "Isabelle Bonnard, only Thérèse calls me Clochette. You know Thérèse, don't you?"

He picked up his stool and walked past several empty sconces to one in which candles were burning. The palace was not nearly so well-lit when the court was gone.

"Don't you?" I asked again.

"I know who she is, of course," he said at last.

"Do you know when the queen returns? Is Saint-Cloud very far away? When will Thérèse come back?"

He climbed onto the stool, replaced the guttered candles, and climbed back down. "I don't know," he said.

He wasn't much use. I sighed. "What do you know, then?"

"I know if you stand on the stage at the opera house and whisper, a person can hear you from the far back row."

The opera house was at the far end of the palace, where Thérèse and I rarely went; I'd never been inside. "Really?"

"Really," he said. His eyes twinkled. "Shall I show you?"

"Please!"

The opera was a vast room, all gilt and pale blue, gloomy in the half-light from the open doors but echoing with whispers just as Pierre had promised. "It was built to celebrate the king's marriage to the queen," he said. "They almost never use it."

"Why ever not?" I knew the queen loved to perform onstage.

Pierre pointed to the enormous chandeliers. "Too expensive," he said. "To light it takes ten thousand candles per night."

Ten thousand candles! As many as Maman and I might use in a hundred years! I looked up at the dark ceiling, trying to imagine it under the bright light of ten thousand flames.

An unwanted thought tugged at the corner of my mind. Was it right? Ten thousand candles at one time?

Next Pierre and I went to the chapel, and then to the long gallery, full of mirrors from floor to ceiling, the most wonderful thing I'd ever seen. "Dance with me," I said to him. He set his stool and basket down, put his heels together, and bowed from the waist. I held up my hands. Together we whirled down the long, long room. A dancing master had been teaching me court dances, and Pierre was quick with his feet. We whirled and stepped, whirled and stepped. Someday, I thought, when I was grown up, this was how I would dance, just like this, at one of the queen's assemblies. I would outshine Ernestine, even Thérèse. All the fair young nobles would beg for my hand.

Pierre stopped in midwhirl. "I'm hungry," he said. "Let's eat."

The palace kitchens were nearly as busy as usual. No one paid any mind to Pierre and me as we helped ourselves to meat off the spit, sweet cakes, and glasses of wine. We ate at one of the long trestle tables that filled the kitchen. Other servants ate there too.

"Is it always this busy?" I asked. "Even when the queen's not here?"

He nodded. "Of course," he said. "We have to eat somewhere, don't we? It takes a lot of servants to run a place this big."

I knew that, of course. "I'm here almost every day," I said. "I play with Madame Royale."

Pierre bit into a cake. "There are over forty candle changers alone. Working full time when the court is here. That's how many candles there are."

"My brother works in the stables," I said. "There are over six hundred horses there."

Pierre nodded. "So. All these people and horses, they have to eat, no matter what." He stretched out his legs. "It's a lucky thing to be the servant of the king. We may not get paid, but we can always eat."

I thought of what George was always saying, that I worked for the queen and didn't get paid. "You are supposed to get a salary, aren't you?" I said. "My brother does, I know."

"Oh, sure," he said. "Four times a year. Only sometimes, you know, the king doesn't have it."

I slipped my hand into my pocket and wrapped my fingers around the king's tiny box, containing the queen's diamond ring. How could the king pay for my ring, if he couldn't pay his servants? And would I get my promised salary, on quarter-day?

For the next several days I made lace in the morning, but left home midafternoon without telling Maman where I was going. I found Pierre, and we romped through the palace together. I saw more of it with him than I ever did with Thérèse. We peeked into the king's rooms, and the Dauphin's. We passed the suites belonging to the king's two brothers, and Pierre whispered to me how fat they were, how gross, how ugly. "But not more so than the king," Pierre said.

I couldn't deny that the king was fat, gross, and ugly, but I said, "He's a kind man. He loves his family."

"Pooh!" said Pierre. "He can't make up his mind. When he has a problem, he frets, he stammers, and then he goes hunting. And going hunting never solves the problem."

Pierre showed me the stairs to the roof, where we ran among the parapets. We could see far across the parkland. As usual, the great fountains stood silent. "My father says he remembers when they ran all the time," Pierre said.

I said, "Thérèse gave me a sheep. I call it Belle-Marie." Beautiful Marie. Like Marie Antoinette, the beautiful queen.

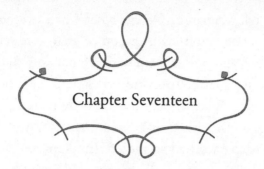

Chapter Seventeen

In a week or two my fun came to an end. I could not say exactly why. Somehow the grand empty palace oppressed me. I began to think about Saint-Cloud. It wouldn't be as grand as Versailles, but I was sure it would still be lavish, and beautiful, and staffed with servants who must live there year-round even if the royal family were in residence only a month.

"All the nobles have large estates," George said.

"But they are hardly ever there," I said. "They spend most of their time at Versailles."

"Of course," George said. "The king wants them where he can see them."

"But that's–" I cut my words off. They would sound disloyal.

"A waste," George finished for me. "What's wrong, Bella?"

"Nothing." But I went back to working full time. In the mornings I made lace for Thérèse. In the afternoons, in the time I would usually have spent at the palace, I made collars and cuffs, small pieces that were easy to sell. Maman couldn't sell them now, of course; with the king and queen away, the nobles had gone back to their own estates. But she set them aside to sell in the fall.

"So, you don't trust the little princess after all?" she asked me.

"I know she will take care of me," I said, "as long as she can."

I did not tell Maman or George what I had overheard on my way downstairs one morning. A group of men were standing near the tavern door, and one of them said, "If that fat fool of a fat king doesn't get off his fat bottom and do something about the price of bread, I'll run a pike through his fat belly myself. My children aren't having another winter like last winter. No, they're not."

I wouldn't have worried so much–drunken men at the tavern always said foolish things–if the man who'd said it hadn't looked so thin, and wolfish, and angry.

I worked to make us a safety net, in the form of pieces of lace. I worked so I wouldn't worry so much, about Thérèse and her papa and their safety, about whether or not she would return to Versailles. I tried to ignore Grand-mère's snores and Maman's complaints; I tried not to complain myself about the heat and the airlessness of our rooms; I tried to not think more than seven or eight times an hour how much I'd rather be playing at Versailles. Then one hot day George showed up and said I must go to Paris with him.

"Of course I can't," I said crossly. "I'm working, as you see. Working hard. Some other time."

"Bella, you know I don't go very often. Today all I'm doing is taking one of the marquis's carriages to his Paris house. I'll be back tonight. Come with me. There are things you should see."

I especially didn't want to go after he said that. I wasn't interested in another of George's lectures. "Oh, come on," he said, pulling my hair the way he used to. "A day out. We'll have fun. Maman, won't she have fun?"

Maman looked up and smiled at me. "Go," she said. "Spend the day with your brother."

I went, but only because Maman made me. The first unpleasant surprise was that George expected me to ride beside him on the outside of the box. "I'm the coachman," he said, surprised at my surprise. "It's my job to drive."

"Can't I sit inside?"

"Of course not! It's not your carriage!" He hoisted me to the box. I pulled my shawl over my head.

"Who do you expect will see you?" he asked. "Everyone you care about is gone."

"The palace servants," I said. "They know me as Thérèse's friend. If they see me they'll laugh at me for riding outside."

"The palace servants," George said, "have better things to do. Two years ago you would have considered a carriage ride into Paris the greatest treat of your life."

I twisted the ring on my finger. "Please do not lecture me. I'm not in the mood."

"I wish you wouldn't wear that in public, Bella. At least turn it so the stone doesn't show."

I turned it so the stone sparkled in the sunlight. George pressed his lips together angrily and was silent. The carriage rolled easily along the smooth road. Before us and in back of us were other fine equipages, carrying courtiers and news away from the palace. Toward us came still more carriages, as well as wagons and farm carts taking food and goods toward the palace and the town. The road between Paris and Versailles was always well traveled, even at this time of year.

"Look at the people in the carts," George said. "Look at their faces. See how thin they are."

I saw that they were ragged, dirty, and unkempt. "Peasants always look like that," I said.

George frowned. "Should they?"

I pulled my shawl over my eyes.

After another mile or so George asked, "Who pays taxes?"

"We do," I said. I meant Maman and Grand-mère, of course. The day the tax collector came was a horrible day; he was a vicious man. I hadn't thought of that. We would have to have cash on hand for him. We must save more money. I would make more lace.

"Yes," George said. "We do, and the farmers do, and the peasants with their tiny plots of land. Wig makers pay taxes, saddlers, chandlers. Anyone who works pays taxes. Tell me, does the bishop?"

How should I know what the bishop did? "Yes?" I guessed. "Yes, he must. He's a very rich man."

Our town priest was not so important, but the priests who said Mass at the palace chapel were grand enough to put the courtiers to shame.

"No. Bishops do not. The church does not. What about the nobles–the dukes and duchesses, your famous friend, Madame de Polignac?"

"I don't know," I said. "How would I know?"

"They don't," George said. "Nor does the Marquis de Lafayette, nor does the king or queen. Nobody at court pays a dime."

"So?"

"So what do you think built the palace? What do you think pays for those fancy dresses you wear, for the parties the queen gives, for that ridiculous diamond you flaunt?"

I didn't say anything.

"People who must work for a living," he said. "People who sometimes can't afford bread to eat. That's who."

"I don't need your lectures," I said. "I understand you very well, George. I don't know what you expect me to do."

We drove the carriage to the marquis's fine Paris home. I pointed out its elegance to George. "The Marquis de Lafayette may love liberty," I said, "but he doesn't feed the peasants."

"He does," George said softly. "He quite often does."

To my horror, we had to walk home. I had assumed some wagon would take us. "You didn't tell me!" I said. "I wouldn't have come."

"It's only twelve miles," George said. "Bella, what's twelve miles? A few hours' walking. Nothing very hard."

"The dust will ruin my shoes," I said.

"Take them off," he told me.

I did take them off. They were delicate slippers, that Thérèse had insisted I take home one day, and they wouldn't have held up to the journey. My feet were scarcely hardier, however. The pebbles hurt.

Dust rolled into our faces every time a wagon rumbled past. I kilted my skirts and walked with my head down. I was furious with George.

Within a few miles I was more exhausted than angry. The sun was hot, and now the muscles in my legs hurt as much as the soles of my feet. My dry throat ached. We had reached the farmland on the outskirts of Paris. George noticed my distress.

"Here," he said, in his old gentle voice. "Ease up a moment, Bella. I'll ask these people for some water."

We had come to a collection of crude huts even dirtier and

more squalid than Ernestine's former home. Pigs rooted in the dirt near the open doorways, and small children sat among the pigs, using sticks to root in the dirt themselves. Fields stretched behind the huts; I could see the bent figures of men and women working there. The wheat was high, its tawny brilliance beautiful in the sun.

A half-grown girl came out of one of the huts, a sickly-looking baby on her hip. George bowed to her and asked politely if we could have some water. She stared us up and down, then nodded and jerked her head toward the well. George drew the pail up and held it for me while I drank. The children watched us warily, like animals.

When we were well on our way down the road again, George said, "Even in a good year, people like that barely survive."

"It must be a good year," I said, thinking of the beauty of that field of wheat.

"Too dry," George said. "Surely you know that. Too dry, the wheat shriveling in its husks. Drought everywhere."

I knew that all summer it had barely rained.

"Even so," he continued, "even in a good year, their cash income goes to pay the tax. They have nothing for themselves. This winter those children will be hungry and cold."

"All right," I said. "They are poor, they are hungry, and the queen is rich and well fed. What do you want me to do? The time I spend at the palace does not take bread from their mouths." I glared at George. "I can't tell the queen what to do."

"No, I know that."

"And besides," I said, pressing my point, "if the queen buys lace from me or from someone else, if she invites me to play with Thérèse or invites some other child, it does not help those people. I might as well make the lace. I might as well be Thérèse's friend. We may as well benefit as anyone else."

"Yes," said George.

"Then what?" I said. "Why did you make me walk so far?"

"I want you to be able to think," he said. "I want you to see more than one side of the world. I want you to know that life at the palace is not everything."

I thought of the queen's soft arms, her scent, her lips brushing my cheek when she saw me. I thought of Maman's worried looks, Grand-mère's kicks. "I already knew that," I said.

I could see the town of Versailles ahead of us when George suddenly asked, "What happened to your shawl?"

In the heat I had been glad not to be carrying it. "I must have dropped it," I said, "when we stopped to drink at the well."

George studied my face. "You dropped it on purpose," he said.

I glared at him, but said nothing. The girl with the baby on her hip had been my own age.

"Well done, Bella," George said. "I see there's hope for you yet." He took my hand and held it the rest of the way home.

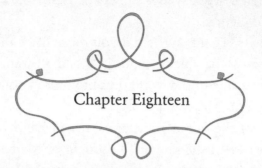

Chapter Eighteen

The royal family and the court returned. I heard the news from the baker one cool morning. Running to the palace, I saw with my own eyes the queen alight from her carriage, and then turn to hover anxiously while two footmen lifted out the small, frail Dauphin. Next came Madame de Polignac, carrying Louis Charles, then Ernestine, and finally Thérèse. She was looking at her mother, but the queen's attention was focused wholly on the poor sick Louis Joseph. He looked worse than ever.

I ran forward. "Thérèse!" I called. "Thérèse!"

Her head snapped up. In the instant before she recognized me, I saw that she was dressed in formal court clothes, an embroidered panniered dress like her mother's, stiff and sumptuous. I had never seen her look so fine. At the same instant, I realized my own plain clothes were covered in dirt. I looked like one of the palace beggars, and I was calling Thérèse by her Christian name. The footmen stared at me. One moved to block my path. Even Madame de Polignac looked astonished. I stopped in my tracks.

Thérèse's face blossomed into the happiest welcoming smile. "Clochette!" she called. She tugged Ernestine's sleeve. "Look, it's Clochette!"

The queen took Thérèse's hand and pulled her toward the door, paying no attention to me or to any of the crowd in the courtyard. She shepherded her children into the palace, away from all the staring eyes. I knew she had to get the Dauphin out of sight quickly, but I couldn't help feeling lost. Then Thérèse stuck her head back out the door. "Come tomorrow!" she shouted, and waved. My heart filled with joy. They were home! Everything would be all right now.

The next afternoon I went to the palace and everything was as it had been before. But George's trip, short though it was, had changed me. I couldn't forget the peasant girl with the baby on her hip. I didn't know if the baby was her brother or her sister or her child. I worried about the winter. George said it would be a hard one with people going hungry after the drought. Would that little baby survive?

The queen's dress book grew larger all the time. The royal dressmaker, the famed Madame Bertin, came twice a week from Paris to show the queen more styles. Sometimes Thérèse and Ernestine and I went to the queen's rooms to watch Madame Bertin unfold lengths of brocade and muslin, silk ribbons, and cloth of gold. The queen would clap her hands with delight.

"Oh, Clochette!" she said one day, holding a piece of cerulean silk against my face. "How beautiful this would be on you! When you are grown up, my dear, we'll make you a court dress of exactly the same color!"

I ran my fingers down the soft glowing cloth. "How much does it cost?" I asked.

A frown flitted over her face, then disappeared. "What a silly question," she said. She turned away, and Madame Bertin glared at me.

"Why can't we speak of what things cost?" I whispered to Ernestine, who shrugged.

"Thérèse," I whispered, "does no one care what the dresses cost?"

Thérèse looked annoyed. *"She is the queen."*

I knew better than to keep asking questions after that, but when Madame Bertin had packed her trunks and gone, the queen turned again to me and said in a low, serious voice, "They criticize me if I don't dress finely enough, you know. A queen must set the style in her country. I love simple gowns, but when I wear them, my ladies say I am not fine enough."

I knew the queen dressed simply when she was at the Hamlet and sometimes at the Trianon, but at the Château she wore several different gowns every day, and most of them were lavish. "But they have no right to criticize you," I said. "You are the queen. You can set the style."

The queen frowned slightly. "Yes, I am the queen. I must look like one. I must be the best dressed at court. Besides–" She laughed her beautiful tinkling laugh. "They are only dresses, my dear. They are not anything so very expensive. A bit of silk, a bit of lace. How much could they be?"

Acres of silk! Miles of lace! "Does she really not know what they cost?" I asked Thérèse as we left.

Thérèse drew up her chin. "I cannot believe you would presume to criticize my mother the queen," she said stiffly. "I don't believe I want you today. Nor tomorrow. Go away."

"I did not mean–"

"I have a headache. Go away."

I went. It was only a few days until quarter-day. I cursed myself for having opened my mouth, for criticizing the queen before we had our quarterly stipend in my hands. What if the queen put a stop to it?

What if Madame de Polignac forgot? What if, as Pierre had said, there wasn't enough money to pay everyone? Winter would come, and we needed to buy fuel. I'd wanted to remind Thérèse of her promise, but now it was too late. I went home and worked until dusk.

"Trouble in paradise?" Maman asked me.

"Thérèse had a headache." After a pause, I asked, "Must the queen dress in finery?" I drew my chair closer to the window. It was a gray, flat evening; I almost wished for a candle to light my work. The lace was so fine it looked like cobwebs.

Maman snorted. "Of course. How else are we to eat?"

"But not quite so fine–not quite so many dresses," I said. "When people are hungry–" Maman had lit a coal fire in our hearth. I wondered if those peasants I had met had wood to burn.

Maman smiled. "You've been talking to George," she said. I nodded. "I'll tell you," Maman said, "this Austrian queen is nothing like queens used to be. She dresses fine, yes, she spends a lot of money, but nothing like a person could hope for. The old king–you won't remember him, he was this king's grandfather–he always had a wife and a girlfriend both. He was always making some new favorite. Then the women would fight for his attention, each trying to be grander than the last. Those were the days to be a lacemaker! Or a wig maker–oh, the fashions they had! Your grandmother used to tell me such stories. Now, though–these last ten years–it's all different. The rivalries so much smaller. This king never looks at any woman but his wife."

"But surely that's better," I said, gasping a little. "The church–"

"Kings are above the church," Maman said, "so long as they make their confession before they die."

I found this so disturbing I let my thread knot. I had to pick it out with the tip of my needle, bending close over the ground cloth. "So they must dress well. But at the same time there is no money, and people are hungry. And the queen buys new dresses twice a week, and never uses the same ribbon twice."

"Such problems are in God's hands," Maman said. "Not ours. Bad enough your brother talks of revolution. You leave well enough alone."

I worked for a while. There was no sound in the room but Grand-mère's snores. She had had another stroke, and now she barely got out of bed. Maman was saving coins for her funeral.

Maman asked in wonderment, "She truly never uses the same ribbon twice?"

"She doesn't like ribbons to have creases in them," I said.

"*Silk* ribbons?" Maman said. "Fresh silk ribbons, every day?"

I nodded. Maman shook her head and made a clucking sound with her tongue. "No wonder your head's been turned," she said.

"Maman," I asked, "where did the money go?"

"What money? We never had money."

"The country's money. Everyone says, 'There's no money *now*.' That means there used to be money."

"The old king spent it," Maman said. "Louis the Fifteenth. And this king, he spends plenty too. And his old aunts, and his cousins and brothers."

"And where did it come from?"

"What?"

"The money. Where did it come from? Whose was it?"

"It was the king's, of course."

"But George said the king pays no taxes. Nor the nobles nor the church."

"Of course not," Maman said. "They never have."

"But–"

"Isabelle," Maman said firmly, "these thoughts will lead to no good. If change comes to France, it will have to come from the king, not the people. The king is the head of France. What God has ordained, men cannot change."

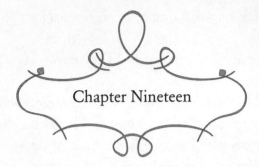

Chapter Nineteen

"I want to see the court," I shouted to Thérèse. We were cantering our ponies across the frozen park. It was winter now; the canals were frozen, so all the boats were taken up, but the ice wasn't yet thick enough for skating. The world was gray and brown; the stone palace, from a distance, blended perfectly into the sky.

Thérèse laughed. "Goose," she said. "This is the court." She took her hand from her reins to wave at a group of elegant men riding in the distance. They bowed to her. "The court," she said. "What did you think it was?"

"I want to see the king and queen eat," I said, "and I want to see a party at night. A ball. And I want to see the queen go to bed."

Thérèse's face lit up. "You'll have to spend the night," she said. "Everyone stays up very late at balls. We won't be allowed, but once the governesses go to sleep we'll use the back halls."

"We should dress up," Ernestine ventured. "We could slip into the crowd and–"

"My mother would see us, right away," said Thérèse.

"We could wear masks," Ernestine said. "Dominos."

"That's brilliant!" said Thérèse. "I'll get some from my mother's maids. But why, Clochette?" I'd never asked to see these things before.

"I just want to watch," I said. "I want to see." Part of me wanted to judge, what could be different, what could change. Part of me wanted to see it all, this grand court, before it was different, before it changed.

I was all set to spend the night at the palace when Grand-mère died in her sleep. Her snoring stopped and she was dead; that was all. I helped Maman lay her out, and I went for the priest and for George. George arranged for the coffin and burial; Maman arranged for the Mass. Many of our neighbors attended, which I thought was kind. I sent a messenger to tell Thérèse, and she sent word back that she and Ernestine would light candles in the palace chapel, for the repose of Grand-mère's soul.

I tried to feel sorrow, but I didn't. I worried, though, about Maman. To my surprise she sobbed throughout the Mass and burial. Days later she still seemed racked by grief.

I could not remember one tender word or touch Grand-mère had ever given me. I could not remember a single kindness from her. I did not understand Maman's feelings.

"She was our family," Maman said. "Your father's mother. Our last tie to him."

I had never felt tied to him, as I didn't remember him at all. I wished I remembered him. I wished I mourned Grand-mère.

"She was different when she was younger," Maman said. "She loved her children. She changed after they all died."

I thought Father had been Grand-mère's only child. When I said so, Maman looked shocked. "But of course," she said, "there was your aunt Elisabeth, who died in childbirth, and your aunt Marie, dead of the plague, and your father's twin, Uncle Robert, who died of dysentery like your father—only not in America, of course. That was the year after you were born. Uncle Robert was the last one—and his wife died the same day."

"I remember Uncle Robert," George said. "Maman always told me to study his face, because it was just like Papa's, and that way I could remember Papa, too."

Now I felt worse—all these phantom aunts and uncles I'd never known existed. I supposed Maman might have had more than a mother and father too—perhaps sisters and brothers, though I'd never asked about them. Now I was afraid to. Who knew what horrible stories I'd hear?

I stayed at home for a week. On my first afternoon back at the palace, Thérèse and Ernestine were gentle with me. They weren't sure how sad I would be.

"I'm sad that I don't feel sad," I told them. "I found out I had aunts and uncles. I never knew."

"Everyone has those," Thérèse said. "How could you not know?"

"No one told me," I said. "They're long dead. Like my father, like most of my family."

Ernestine squeezed my hand in sympathy. Thérèse didn't really understand. "Dead relatives cannot be as important as live ones. Some of Maman's brothers and sisters are dead, you know, and then the families they married into aren't tied to us anymore. It's the ones that are still alive that count."

"Mine count, dead or alive," I said.

"But your relatives are different from mine, Clochette. Neither you nor Ernestine can really understand." Thérèse was acting the Princess Royale now, which was hard to bear. "It will be different for you," she continued. "When you are my ladies, you will marry well, and your children will have connections.

"My family are the Holy Roman Emperor, and the queen of Naples, and Archduke Maximilian–he came visiting once–you've heard me talk of them, I know."

"I suppose." I couldn't stop Thérèse blathering, but I didn't have to sound enthusiastic.

"Maman says we don't need to worry," Thérèse confided. Her voice dropped to a whisper. "Sometimes, you know, we hear rumors–about people rising against us. Revolution. Partially because of the Estates-General. But Maman knows nothing bad can happen to us, because of all her brothers and sisters. Come. Let us walk in the gardens."

As we went out, Ernestine again squeezed my hand. "I'm sorry for your troubles, Clochette," she whispered, and I hugged her.

George explained that the Estates-General Thérèse spoke of was a meeting of delegates from the three states of France–the nobility, the clergy, and the commoners. It was going to take place next summer, here at Versailles. The king had called for it, the first such meeting in a hundred and seventy-five years.

"It's a radical thing to do," George said. "It means the king might actually ask for reform. The trouble is, he's not likely to get it. Each state gets one vote as a whole. You know, one vote for the nobles, one vote for the clergy, and one for everyone else. So the commoners don't actually have a voice–the nobles and clergy can overrule anything they like."

"But if the clergy and the nobles agree that something must change–"

"Why would they want change?" George asked. "They are comfortable now."

Despite the rumbles of discontent I heard in the marketplace as winter grew colder, despite my own worries about the starving peasants, I didn't understand why Thérèse seemed so concerned.

"What are you afraid of?" I asked. It was treason to *speak* ill of the king, much less to threaten his royal person. I had not forgotten the drunken man at the tavern, but I worried more because he sounded so desperate for his family than because I thought he might be able to actually do any harm.

"I'm afraid because Maman is afraid," Thérèse answered. "Maman is afraid because Papa is not afraid, and she thinks he should be. I don't want to talk about it, Clochette."

I still didn't really understand, but I knew better than to press Thérèse. Were they afraid of giving up luxuries? Of not having quite so many palaces, quite so many beautiful gowns? Quite so many courtiers jostling for a glimpse of them, begging for a favor?

Then one day as I was leaving, the candle boy Pierre stopped me in the hall. Our hours together over the summer had made us friends, and now I often waved to him and he sometimes winked at me as he made his rounds with the candles. I had given him a handful of nuts once, from the dinner table, and he had given me a candle stub to take home to Maman.

Now he said, "Here," and pressed a paper into my palm. "This is what they're saying about your queen."

"She's your queen too," I said. He shrugged. I smoothed the paper, then held it toward the candles so that light fell on it.

"Oh," I said. "Oh, *no*. How awful." My voice shook. I couldn't read, but I understood the picture on the printed sheet. It showed the queen as a harpy, a wicked marauding creature with wings and claws and a great harsh beak. It looked like the queen, and yet it also looked like a harpy, like evil come to life.

"For shame!" I hissed at Pierre. "To show me such trash! To bring it into the palace!"

He looked at me steadily. "I didn't bring it into the palace," he said. "I found it here. Pinned up onto a wall. They're being printed in Paris by the thousands, you know. All sorts of pamphlets, and all against the queen."

"It's not right," I said. "It's not her fault."

"Isn't it?" Pierre looked away. "I don't blame you for defending her, after she's made such a pet of you–but everyone says there's no money, no food, no bread. The country's falling apart, and the king could do something, and he doesn't."

"The king, perhaps. Not the queen."

"Except that everyone knows he does everything she says."

I didn't know if that was true or not–I rarely saw the king–but I didn't care. "You should not show me such trash," I repeated.

"I thought you should know," he said. "The country's in the hands of an Austrichienne. She'll destroy us all."

I pushed past him, down the wide hall. It was filled as it always was with dozens of well-dressed courtiers, all dressed in bright silks and brocades, all waiting for a brief glimpse of the king or queen. The women's powdered wigs towered above their heads. The men's jackets dripped gold lace. Above everything rose the stench of unwashed bodies. Not a thing had changed as far as I could see.

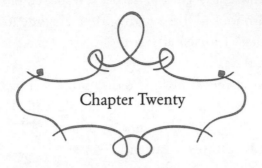

Chapter Twenty

"It's worse," George said. "I could take you to the countryside and prove it, if I had the time." He pitched hay from a stall into a barrow while he spoke to me. They had cut the number of servants working in the stables. George worked all the time now. "Of course people are angry," he continued. "They are cold, they are starving, and still they must pay tax so that rich men can wear velvet and play games without care."

"But it's not the queen's fault," I said. I had told him about the horrible pamphlet.

"Perhaps not. But people blame her. Those pamphlets are everywhere, all over Paris. They accuse her of all sorts of things. Of improper relations, lasciviousness, buying jewels that will bankrupt the nation. Some call her Iscariot. Others, Madame Deficit."

"She does not have improper relations. She is perfectly chaste. She does not spend money on jewels."

George paused for a moment, then resumed his work. "Maybe not. But if you were starving, or Maman was, you might blame her for it too."

Now at last the day came when I was to stay the night at the palace, and see a ball. The ball was our secret, of course, Thérèse's and Ernestine's and mine.

First, that day, we went to the king's dinner. I had often thought of going before, but Thérèse and her household ate at the same time, and anyhow, Thérèse said it made her stomach hurt.

"Because you're hungry?" I said. "We can eat early, can't we?"

"Not that," she said.

I didn't understand until I saw it for myself. The king sat at one end of a huge gilded table. The queen sat at the other, far away. Before they came in, however, a host of courtiers all dressed in their finest crowded around the edge of the room. Most of them stood. Servants brought out folding stools for a few of the duchesses, and then brought one for Thérèse, though not for Ernestine or me. Madame de Polignac made sure we were able to stand at the front of the crowd. More and more people pushed in.

When the king came in, he did not make eye contact with anyone, but he looked happy. He settled himself into a fine gilt armchair and waited for a servant to spread a napkin across his lap. The queen slipped into her chair with her eyes down. She looked uncomfortable, even angry. Neither one of them noticed Thérèse.

As soon as the king and queen sat, footmen began to carry in serving dishes full of food, shouting as they shouldered their way through the crowds. They offered each dish to the king and queen, and then set the dish on the table.

I had become accustomed to the magnificence of Thérèse's table, but the king's table was much finer. The serving dishes, and plates, and forks and spoons, were made of elaborately worked gold. Dish after dish until they covered the table. The wonderful food smells made my stomach rumble.

The king piled his plate high and ate with enthusiasm. The queen seemed to hunch her shoulders against the crowd. She refused most of the offered dishes. When she finally allowed a servant to put a few spoonfuls of what looked like venison on her plate, she tasted it, and shook her head. "Cold," she said with disgust. "Can nothing be brought hot to this table?"

The kitchens were a very long way from the dining room.

That was all the queen said during the entire meal. She never spoke to the king, nor the king to her. Whenever she lifted her fork to her lips, dozens of courtiers and commoners–any man dressed in a hat and sword, any woman at all–watched her chew. They stared while she swallowed, stared while she sipped from the glass of wine by her plate.

Ernestine and I stared. Thérèse looked at her parents as though willing them to turn their heads and acknowledge her. After a while she gave up and stared at her hands.

By the end of the meal I'd counted thirty-seven dishes on the table. Many had not been touched. The queen had eaten venison, rabbit, a small white roll, and something that looked like stewed fruit. That was all. The king had refilled his plate several times.

When both had finished, the king and queen got up without ceremony, and abruptly walked out. The courtiers followed in a stream, calling "Your Majesty! Your Majesty!" as they hurried down the hall.

Thérèse stood, and a servant took away her stool. "Do you see why I hate it?" she said.

I tried to imagine my own mother on display like this, not

just sometimes, but every single day. I tried to imagine sitting in the queen's chair, the center of all that strange attention. "I see," I said.

The king's dinner was horrid, but the ball was like a fairy tale.

I had been to the Hall of Mirrors before, but only in the daytime. Nothing prepared me for the glittering glory of the room at night.

At any time, the hall was extraordinary, the most beautiful and elaborate room in the palace. All along one long side, arches framed tall windows looking out onto the gardens. All along the other side, matching marble arches framed walls of solid mirrors.

There was never anything richer in the world. We owned a mirror at home, of a size that would fit in your hand; it was one of our treasures, and Grand-mère used to hide it from me for fear I would break it. Mirrors were made of silver–silver on the back of the smoothest glass that blowers could fashion. The smallest dimple in the glass, or fleck in the silver, made a bad spot in a mirror. And here were seventeen arches, three feet wide and fifteen feet high, with mirrors like windowpanes filling all that vast space, not a fleck, not a ripple in the glass.

Crystal chandeliers hung from the painted vaulted ceiling. Bronze statues held up crystal sconces. Gold-covered tables flanked marble statues resting in niches all along the walls.

That was the hall in daytime. Now, in her dark room, Thérèse giggled and lit a candle and led Ernestine and me through a labyrinth of back hallways.

"Where are we going?" whispered Ernestine.

"Shh!"

I couldn't believe no one was stopping us. We had not waited that long after going to bed before rising and stealthily slipping into our gowns. We had dominos, silk masks that covered our heads, but our dresses were ordinary; Thérèse's fine court clothes were kept packed away, and we had not been able to come up with an excuse for the servants to get them out.

The back halls and stairways were far from empty, but no one paid attention to us. We passed a dozen servants–and more than a few courtiers who wanted to move around the palace unseen.

Ernestine stopped. Her face glowed in the candle's light. "Listen!" she said. I strained my ears. *Violin music,* I thought. Dancing. I squeezed Thérèse's hand.

Thérèse led us up a dark steep stairway and carefully opened a small panel door. She peeked inside, then turned back to us. I could see her wide smile. "I wanted to show you this first," she said.

We stepped into a vast golden room. A branch of lit candles flickered on a tabletop. A guard near the fire stood up to look at us, but when Thérèse pulled off her domino, he laughed and waved his hand.

In front of us stood a huge bed hung with cloth of crimson and gold. "Come, look," Thérèse said, tugging me to one side. She opened a door with a window in it, and we stepped outside onto a balcony.

We were in the exact center of Versailles. The balcony overlooked the heart of the main courtyard, the Marble Court, which was filled now with elegant carriages bringing still more courtiers to the ball. We watched them for a moment, then slipped back into the room. I knew where we were. The king's bedchamber.

"Come," whispered Thérèse. She brushed aside one of the hangings behind the bed. There, not surprisingly, was a narrow door. Thérèse eased it open.

We were in the exact center of the Hall of Mirrors. The door we had come through *was* one of the mirrors–mirrored on one side.

Ernestine and I gasped in unison. The room looked like a field of diamonds, spun through with gold. Every chandelier and every sconce shone with the light of a dozen candles; each of the thousand flames flickered through the crystal baubles and reflected over and over in that solid wall of mirrors.

The court was nothing compared to the room. The court was just as it always was, glittering velvet, embroidery and lace, jewels and wigs and hooped skirts and lice.

The room was alive and enchanting.

Thérèse closed the mirrored door and we stood with our backs to it, watching. Musicians played, and men and women danced. The candles and the heat of bodies made the room quite warm. "Shall we dance?" whispered Thérèse.

We had been taught court dances. "With each other?" Ernestine whispered.

"No–ask someone!"

"Thérèse!" It was impossible for a woman, let alone a girl, to ask a man to dance. And no man would ask us–in our dominos and plain dresses, we were as invisible as the shadows in the room.

Anyway, I did not wish to dance. I searched the glittering room, hoping for a glimpse of the queen. There she was, in a wide, extravagant gown cut away to reveal layer after layer of lace-trimmed underskirt. Her hair was her own, not as immense as some of the wigs, but powdered and pouffed and run through with pearls.

I saw her at the same time as she saw us. Her eyes widened, and her mouth grew firm. I could tell that she recognized us. I elbowed Thérèse to warn her.

The queen sailed toward us, courtiers moving out of her way

like rowboats giving way to a ship. She did not look happy. I knew we were in for a scold.

But when the queen was partway across the room, the king appeared at her side. She spoke a few quick words to him, and he glanced our way. His eyes narrowed–I knew he could not see well–and then his face split into a grin. He patted the queen on the arm, laughing, and came up to us.

"Madame," he said, inclining his head to his daughter.

Thérèse curtsied deeply. "Your Majesty." Through the domino I could see her eyes sparkle.

"Shall we dance?" The king held out his arm. Thérèse took it with a little skip. They moved to the center of the floor. The musicians struck up a new tune, and the court seemed to hold its breath. The king danced awkwardly, with little feeling for the rhythm of the music, but Thérèse was lithe and graceful, and her happiness transfigured the king. Ernestine and I watched hand in hand.

"This is only our first ball," I said. "In a few years we will be ladies, and the men of the court will line up for the privilege of a dance."

Ernestine gave a tiny shake of her head, and I wished I hadn't spoken. There was no reason to mar this perfect moment with talk of a future we no longer trusted.

Chapter Twenty-one

Spring came, and with it my third quarter-day as lacemaker to Thérèse. I went to the offices of Thérèse's household, and the man there solemnly counted into my hands two hundred and fifty livres. They were heavy to carry; they filled a cloth sack. "So," George said drily, as I stepped out of the room. "You're still on the books, I see."

He had come to walk me home, to protect me and the money, and I was grateful for that. No one in the town knew we were paid quarterly; it would be too much temptation to rob us. "I do my job," I said.

"I know you do," he said. "You walk a fine line, Bella. Many days I admire you."

I smiled at him. "*And* I make fine lace," I said.

"And you make fine lace," he agreed.

It was March. The last months had been terribly cold, with bitingly cruel winds and much snow. With Thérèse and Ernestine I had ice-skated on the frozen canals and sledged through the parkland; with Maman I had shivered in our drafty room and worried about the rising price of firewood. Today the first hint of warmth in the air felt like a blessing, and I was glad.

Maman had overcome her grief, and could be happy again. Without Grand-mère to feed, we could afford laudanum whenever Maman needed it, and we'd made it through the winter in fine shape. Maman's hands hurt a little less than before.

But the country had grown angrier over the winter, until you could feel the anger pressing right up against the gates of the palace. The king's advisers came and went, but nothing changed that I could see. "That's because," George said bitterly, "the king is doing all he can to do nothing at all. He won't do *anything*. Soon it won't matter. It will be too late."

"But when the Estates-General comes to Versailles?"

George considered. "The town will be overrun, there won't be an empty bed at the palace, everyone will eat and drink too much, and nothing will be accomplished."

"Something will," I said.

"Something, someday, soon," he said, "but not because of the Estates-General. Either the king will summon the courage to make difficult decisions–which I doubt–or someone with courage will begin to make decisions for him."

"But you support the king, don't you?" I asked him.

He looked away.

"George," I said, "promise me you won't do anything to harm the king. You must promise."

Finally he looked at me. "I won't hurt him, Bella."

"You won't do anything against him. Promise me."

"I will do what I think is right, Bella. That's the best I can do."

We walked on in silence, our heads bent a little against the still-chilly wind. I tried not to think of the implications of George's words. "Thérèse says that nothing bad can happen to them," I said. "She says the Holy Roman Emperor, her mother's brother, will protect them, and so will the other heads of state."

George seemed to choose his next words with great care. "Except that some countries might prefer a different king of France," he said. "They have to do business with France, and so it might be that they would prefer a king who can make decisions. One who actually leads his people. Someone like the king's brother, perhaps. Or his cousin, the Duke of Orléans."

I thought about this. "You're saying you're not sure the emperor would help the queen, even though the queen is his sister?"

George shrugged. "I'm not sure of anything. What I hear sounds dangerous. Be careful, Bella. I wish you weren't at the palace every day."

Thérèse's brother, the frail Dauphin, was near death. We all knew this, and the knowledge hung around us like a funeral pall. The queen spent hours tending him; her eyes were heavy from lack of sleep, and her face was sad deep down in a way that nothing could reach. But her face brightened a little whenever she saw Thérèse or the little Duke of Nomandy, and her smile reached her lips if not her eyes.

One day at the palace Thérèse said, "You promised me you would always stay with me. You are to be one of my ladies. No matter what happens. Remember, you promised."

We were walking through the park, full of flowers again, and leaves, and courtiers dressed in silks and satin. "I promise," I said. "You know that. Why do you remind me?"

"I just want to," she said. "I must know I can trust you. Royal persons must know whom they can trust."

Ernestine and I both stopped still. "Thérèse," Ernestine said, "when could you ever not trust us?"

Thérèse's face trembled a bit. "One never knows," she said.

"You do," I said. I put my arm through hers. I hated to see her looking so pale and anxious. "Why do you worry?"

"Why not?" she said. "My brother can hardly sit up now. My mother weeps and refuses to be part of the court. My father is king by divine right, by the will of God, but sometimes I hear–even I, his own daughter–hear murmurings against him." She waved her hand toward a group of nobles walking on the path far ahead of us, and I saw that it included her uncle, the Count of Artois. "Do you know? I don't believe those men want to obey him. Not any of them. And yet they must. It is the will of God."

I wanted to say that people could only obey a king who actually gave commands, but I did not. I didn't want to distress Thérèse further. And she was right: Her father had been born king, not raised there. He was king by God's will. It was wrong to turn against him.

Or was it?

If a king was unjust, was it wrong to turn against him? The Americans had turned against the English king and won their freedom. My father had been part of that, as servant to the marquis. The marquis believed in freedom so much that he had sailed his own ship to America, and fought there himself.

Was it right, or was it wrong?

Thérèse, of course, could see only one side. She was Princess Royale by divine right, or so she believed. She had no reason to wish her life to be changed.

The month of May came, and it was time for the meeting of the Estates-General.

Thérèse trembled with indignation at the very idea. "It's an injustice. An absolute injustice. He is king of all France, and now he has to *negotiate*. Bah! Especially with the Third Estate!" she hissed. "Why would they have any rights in the government? It's not as if they even own land!"

We were shut up in Thérèse's rooms, because she was too upset to go outside. She didn't want, she said, to see so many commoners lurking around the royal gardens. The town was packed with delegates, and the ones who were not usually part of the court roamed the palace with disbelieving eyes.

"The peasants do too own land," I retorted. "George told me."

"Oh, bah!" said Thérèse.

"I bet Ernestine's family does."

Ernestine sighed and shook her head. My arguments with Thérèse caused her anxiety.

"See?" said Thérèse.

"Well, but the Third Estate pays all the taxes. The nobles and clergy don't."

Thérèse's mouth screwed up and her eyes blazed. "That's how it should be! That is how it has always been! This talk of no money is ridiculous. Of course there is money! There has always been money!"

"On my first day here," I said, "you yourself told me the fountains didn't run all the time because there was no money."

"No money for the fountains!" she said. "What use are fountains? There's plenty of money for other things!"

As always, I was torn. "People are starving. I saw them myself.

And that was before this horrible winter. Thérèse–"

"It's not my father's fault." She had tears in her eyes. Thérèse, who was too strong to ever cry. "Jesus said, 'The poor you will always have with you.' There will always be poor people, and rich ones. My father does the best he can. He is king because it is God's will."

"Ernestine and I are part of the Third Estate," I said. I tried hard not to show how frustrated I was. Thérèse was so frightened, and I owed her so much. But why did she remain blind?

"You and Ernestine!" Thérèse said. "Women have no rights. And you are *not* part of the Third Estate. You are my ladies, and as soon as I can, I will give you both titles."

"I don't need a title," I said. "I will serve you well without one. My brother is part of the Third Estate, and always will be."

"God's will," she hissed.

I tried to be very gentle, but I had to say some small part of the truth. "Some people disagree. Some people think our lives should not be completely determined by who our parents are."

Thérèse turned from me, shoulders rigid and jaw tight. Then her shoulders began to shake. Ernestine put her arm around Thérèse, and after a moment I, too, put my hand on her shoulder. She looked at me. "I know," she whispered. "Papa says no one knows what will happen now. No one knows what we should do."

Chapter Twenty-two

On the fourth of May the delegates of the Estates-General paraded into Versailles in solemn triumph. They went in order, the Third Estate, the Second, the First, and finally the king and queen, the queen in cloth of silver, the king in cloth of gold. Marie Antionette had wanted the Dauphin with her, carried in a litter, but he was too weak even for that.

Thérèse and Ernestine and I watched from the windows of Maman's apartment. When I realized that the procession would be going right past our apartment, I had, with some trepidation, invited Thérèse to my home.

At first she had looked puzzled. "Your home?" she said.

"We live on the first floor, above the tavern," I said. "You'd be out of the crowds, but you could see everything." No one had suggested that Thérèse march, even though she was the king's oldest child. Girls were not important to the throne.

The queen gave permission, so long as we were careful and discreet, and took Madame de Polignac and some of the under-governesses. "Though why you want to see such a thing, I don't know," she said fretfully. "I would skip it if I possibly could."

The king's advisers had said absolutely that the king and queen must march. Already so much of the Third Estate was against them; if they did not show respect by marching in the procession, no one would pay attention to a word the king said.

The queen and Thérèse approved my plan, but Maman did not. "Bring Madame Royale here!" she said. "Are you out of your mind? What shall we serve her? Where shall she sit? We have nothing fine enough for that one. My goodness, Isabelle, how can you be so blind?"

"She wants to see the procession," I said. "This is the best way. She won't mind. Our chairs are good enough."

Except that they weren't. Maman and I spent the evening scouring our floors and chasing all the dust and cobwebs out of the corners. We waxed the top of the table and set out flowers from the marketplace, and freshened the bed and made sure the chamber pots were emptied and clean. Maman bought some wine, and some fresh-baked bread, and even a bunch of grapes, to have something to offer Thérèse. Our rooms looked as fine as they ever had.

Not long after breakfast a small coach pulled up to our door. Thérèse and Ernestine alighted, and then Madame de Polignac and two servants. One of the servants carried a small gilded chair. She moved one of our straight-backed chairs away from the window, and set the gilded chair down for Thérèse.

Thérèse greeted me with an awkward kiss and a somewhat distracted smile. "They've taken my brother the Dauphin to Meudon, to his own palace there," she said. "Because of the noise and the crowds."

"Is he better?" I asked.

"No." She went to the palace chair and sat down, and calmly spread her skirts and adjusted her seat so she would have a good view. She did not ask to be introduced to my mother, who hovered near the door. Of course, I reminded myself, she had met my mother before.

Maman offered wine all around. Madame de Polignac settled in one of our chairs next to Thérèse, and after a pause Ernestine and I stood at the other window. There was only one chair left, and I would not sit in it while my mother stood, and neither, it appeared, would Ernestine.

Below us, crowds of commoners lined the street to see the show. First came those selected to represent the Third Estate, most of them wealthy Paris merchants, all dressed in solemn black with tricorne hats. They marched respectfully, but as they were going past, Thérèse cried, "Oh, that traitor!" and leapt from her seat. Her hands clutched the windowsill. Her eyes widened and grew dark. "How dare he! Oh, I hate him!"

Still I saw nothing irregular about the lines of black-garbed men. Ernestine and I went to Thérèse's side.

"That one!" she said, pointing. "The king my father's cousin!"

"Philippe, the Duke of Orléans," said Madame de Polignac. "He's calling himself Philippe Egalité." Philippe Equality.

A prince of the royal blood, marching not with the nobles, as was his right–as was his duty–but with the commoners in the Third Estate. "He's pretending to be a friend of the peasants," said Thérèse.

A traitor. The Duke of Orléans–Philippe Egalité–was trying to look like both royalty and a common man.

Until that moment, I hadn't really understood the danger that the king was in. I hadn't understood all George had said. I had thought that people wanted the king to make different decisions, to spend his money on the poor, to treat his people more fairly. Now–my heart beat fast for Thérèse–I knew better. People wanted to be governed by someone other than the king.

We watched the nobles go by beautifully attired in satin, silk, and lace, and then the clergy, the parish priests dressed simply, the bishops and abbots in beautiful robes, and finally the king and queen with painted-on smiles and pained eyes. After the procession was over–but before the delegates descended on Versailles in a meat-eating, wine-drinking horde–Thérèse and Ernestine returned to the palace. The queen, Thérèse said, was going to Meudon to be with the Dauphin as quickly as she could. After the king's opening speech he was going to Meudon too, though only for the night since the negotiations of the Estates-General would begin the next day.

The Dauphin died that night.

It had been a hot night with no wind. I had been worried about the Dauphin and about Thérèse, and had lain sleepless on my bed while the moon rose, flooding the room with moonlight, and then set, putting it into darkness. I finally dozed off as the sky was beginning to turn rose pink, and I woke not much later to the tolling of bells.

I jumped out of bed. Nobody had to tell me what the bells meant. "I must go to Thérèse," I said, and began to dress.

Maman handed me a mug of cider. "Is little Madame Royale always as sad as she was yesterday?" she asked me.

"Thérèse?" I gulped the cider. "She was so worried. She loved him."

Maman patted my shoulder. "The next one is healthier, yes? It will be all right."

"Maman?" I said. "That business yesterday, with the chair–I'm sure Thérèse didn't mean to snub you. Royals always have to sit in a finer chair than anyone else." I had worked this out for myself while I lay awake in the night.

"Yes, yes," Maman said. "I told you we had nothing fine enough for her here. I was glad she brought that chair."

"The next one," little Louis Charles, slipped his hand into mine as I came into Thérèse's rooms. "My brother died," he said to me. "Now I'm Dauphin."

I knew he was not being cruel. He was only four years old. I knelt down and hugged him. "He went to heaven to live with Jesus," I said.

"That's right," Louis Charles said. His blond curls bobbed as he nodded. "That's what Madame de Polignac says. He went away, but he'll be back."

"That's not–" He was already gone, running out the tall open doors to look at some horsemen in the woods.

"It doesn't matter," Thérèse said softly. She had come up behind me.

I put my arms around her, and kissed her cheek. "He's too little," I said.

"He'll understand eventually." She had been crying, but her eyes were dry now. She held herself perfectly erect, in a dress of absolute black, and I was ashamed for my own gray dress even though it was the most somber of the few dresses I had at home. I hurried to change. The servants had thrown together black dresses for both Ernestine and me. They took all our other dresses away to be dyed black. We would mourn the little prince for a year.

The Estates-General did not mourn him for more than a day. As soon as the funeral Mass was sung, the delegates began to grumble. Where was the king? Why was he not attending to his duty? He came and sat among us in the queen's rooms at the palace, his head bowed with grief. He sobbed unashamedly. When one of his ministers whispered something about the Estates, he said bitterly, "Are there no fathers among the Third Estate?"

I did not go home. I sent word to Maman that I was staying at the palace for as long as Thérèse needed me. The gardens were not pleasant with so many people about, so we stayed shut up in her hot, stinking rooms. We embroidered and practiced our dancing, and Ernestine and I tried to be cheerful.

After three more days the king took up his chair at the meeting, and the negotiations began. They went nowhere. "Worthless," George said, shaking his head when I snuck out to see him that night. We could not get reliable news inside the palace. The servants seemed reluctant to tell us anything.

"All they've done so far is stir up malcontent," said George. "Everything the Third Estate suggests gets voted down by the nobles and the clergy, who won't give an inch of their rights." He sighed. "They refuse to pay taxes. They don't want reform. The Third Estate expected better treatment. They're getting really mad, and I for one don't blame them."

Days passed like this. The king could not convince anyone to change. People shouted and shook their fists; they started fights in town. George told me that he was sleeping at home each night, and that Maman barred our door with a thick piece of oak. Meanwhile horrible pamphlets flooded Versailles, accusing the queen of sending all the country's money to her brother the emperor. Some said she got drunk every night–the queen, who never touched more than a sip of wine!

"Lies," Thérèse said, weeping.

"All lies," I said to George.

"What good is the truth?" asked George.

I saw what he meant. People would believe what they wanted to believe. The country was sliding out of the king's hands.

On June twentieth I was still at the palace, sitting with Thérèse and Ernestine and the grieving queen. When a group of the king's ministers rushed in, calling for the king, the queen got up to join them, leaving us alone.

"Go to your brother," Thérèse told me. "He'll know what's going on."

I hurried through the courtyard to the stables. All the vast space was filled with the cheering of raucous crowds of men. At the stables George was working just as always, flinging manure into a wheelbarrow, but his eyes sparkled with excitement and he seemed taller.

"They did it!" he said. "The Third Estate walked out. They met on their own, at a tennis court, and they declared themselves separate from the king. They *voted* to declare themselves separate. It's started, Bella! Our revolution!"

"All of them voted?" I could not quite believe that the entire Third Estate were against the king.

"All of them," said George. "And lots of the low-ranking clergy–the priests, you know, not the bishops–and forty-seven members of the nobility, too!"

"Philippe Egalité," I said bitterly.

"Yes, him," said George. "They're calling themselves the National Assembly. They're going to be a new government–not ruled by the king. They will act upon the will of the people.

We're going to be able to vote, Bella! All the members of the National Assembly will vote."

"You're going to vote?"

"Not me, of course not. They'll work out who votes. But it's a whole new beginning"–George could not keep the excitement out of his voice–"a new system, like in America. Or England, with their Parliament. The marquis approves."

The Marquis de Lafayette, the defender of liberty. "But he's the king's friend!"

"Yes," George said, smiling and confident, "and he's the head of the assembly. He loves liberty, *and* he loves the king. He'll make sure this turns out right."

Back at the palace, sitting with Thérèse in the queen's library, I could hear the king rage. I had never heard him so much as raise his voice before. "I'll send troops!" he roared. "Kill them all, if they don't back down!"

They didn't back down. They threatened the king. All Paris supported the assembly, or so the assembly said, and a mob of thirty thousand people would attack Versailles, unless the king gave way.

He yielded. He had no choice.

The new National Assembly returned to Paris to start the government. The nobles, incredibly, resumed their games at Versailles. They hunted and gambled and danced as though nothing had changed. I couldn't believe it. The atmosphere in the palace was different, edgy and anxious, but still the king hunted and the courtiers crowded his dining room to watch him eat. The queen withdrew to the Trianon and began to rehearse another play.

I thought I should go home, but Thérèse and Ernestine begged me to stay. Both of them had begun having nightmares, while I stayed awake long into the night.

"You must stay with me," Thérèse said. "You promised."

"Please get away from there," George said, when I went to ask him to tell Maman. "Quit pretending you are royalty. For your own sake, stay away."

"Why?" I asked. "Do you know something I don't? Is Thérèse in danger?"

"No," he said. "Don't look at me that way. If I knew of anything afoot, I'd get you out of there whether you liked it or not." He shook his head. "I drove to Paris with the marquis. People there are unhappy–more than unhappy. Inflamed."

"They got what they wanted," I said. "They stole the king's authority."

He looked serious. "I don't think that's all they want. As for stealing–is it wrong to steal, to save your life?" He leaned on his pitchfork. "You know the king has stationed troops all around Versailles."

I knew this. I liked seeing them when we rode out into the park. I felt safer with them around.

"Most of them are foreign mercenaries, not Frenchmen," George continued. "The king's got them in Paris, too. If he's so loved by his people, why is he ready to attack them?"

"He's defending himself," I said.

George shook his head. "You don't need that many troops to defend yourself."

It was foolishness, foolishness all around. No one could say what would happen next. "I know," Thérèse said one morning. "Let's plan a special luncheon for the queen."

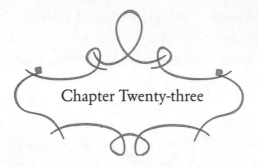

Chapter Twenty-three

A party for the queen was no less foolish, I supposed, than the king going hunting every day. The queen was still so sad over the Dauphin that anything that cheered her must have been a good thing. And I knew it was better for Thérèse to get out of the palace for a little while, and have something to occupy her mind.

The queen's favorite place at Versailles was the Petit Trianon. My favorite place, and Ernestine's, was the Hamlet.

It was like a little village, with a dairy, a fishery, some pretty little houses, a dovecote, and a water mill, all nestled together in a section of the palace parkland. Marie Antoinette had had it built just a few years before. It reminded her, she said, of the happy country days of her childhood in Austria, and besides, model villages were all the rage among the nobles. The queen loved to have us play there, among the pretty cows and the sheep.

My favorite cow there was named Blanche. I often milked her myself, and the farmer who ran the Hamlet helped me skim the milk into a beautiful porcelain jar. Then my milk would be taken to the palace, and we would drink it from crystal glasses while it was still warm.

"Let's *cook* for her," I said.

Thérèse giggled at the absurdity of that. "We'll do everything ourselves."

This would not have been possible at the palace, or even at the Trianon, but here in the Hamlet, the servant family all gave way to us in whatever we asked. The farmer's son rowed us out to the center of the pond, and helped us catch fish for our meal. The farmer showed us how to grind wheat into flour at the mill, and his wife taught us to make the flour into dough for bread. We picked flowers and decorated the little dining room in the queen's house at the Hamlet.

Thérèse supervised the rest of the menu. Ernestine laid the table with pretty, simple china plates. We had everything ready by the time Her Majesty pulled up in her open carriage, and we rushed out to meet her.

She was dressed as she always was when she came to the Hamlet, in a plain white muslin dress and a large straw hat. Madame Le Brun had painted her dressed like this the year before. I had heard courtiers scoff at the painting–"She doesn't look royal. She looks like a servant."–but I loved it. It showed the queen as I liked her best.

Besides, she never acted like a servant, no matter how she was dressed. She was still every inch a queen.

Thérèse was no longer as stiff around her mother. Either the Dauphin's death, or the encroaching atmosphere of danger, or both, had softened her. That day, at the Hamlet, she made a great story of how we had caught the fish. The queen laughed and laughed–the first time I had heard her laugh in months. Ernestine glowed, and I felt full of happiness.

"We did everything ourselves," Thérèse boasted.

"Except for the rowing," I said. "And also baiting the hook.

And taking the fish off the line, and gutting it, and removing the scales. And frying it."

Thérèse rolled her eyes at me. "We caught the fish," she said. "We did everything."

"Splendid!" said the queen. "Well done!" She raised her glass to us. "A toast," she said, "to my three favorite young ladies, three jewels of France."

George spat in disgust when I told him about it. "The country is falling to pieces, so you decided to have a luncheon?" he said. "You've become like them, Bella. Worthless, frivolous."

I spat back, and glared at him. "You didn't scoff at Maman when she was mourning Grand-mère," I said, "and Grand-mère was her horrible old mother-in-law, not her little child. You're the one who can't see straight now. Giving someone happiness is never evil, nor is comforting someone in their grief."

"I don't object to you comforting the queen," he said. "But that ridiculous Hamlet–take that pretend village and compare it to any actual farm you've ever seen. Real cows aren't bathed with expensive soap and scented with perfume, Bella. They aren't milked into porcelain bowls. So long as the queen thinks that farm life is anything like her pretend world, she's going to be blind to our country's problems."

"I don't think she's blind," I said. "She likes to playact, that's all."

"She has no business acting while France is falling apart."

"I thought you were happy about this revolution," I said.

"I am. But if we're going to move peacefully to both a parliament and a king, we need the royal family to show some sense."

The weather took an awful turn just a few days later. I had gone back to sleeping at home, and I spent the morning trying to make lace in the dim light. Rain fell steadily as I hurried to the palace. It was very cold, even though it was now the middle of July.

The queen was sitting with Thérèse and Ernestine when I arrived. All three of them embraced me.

"Can you spend the night tonight?" Thérèse asked right away.

"I suppose so," I said, "if we can send a servant to tell Maman."

"Oh, good!" she said.

"Good," agreed Ernestine, "though I'm sure all this fuss is about nothing."

She said this with a careful glance at the queen. I didn't know what Ernestine meant. I wasn't aware of any fuss. The town had seemed quiet when I'd walked through it, the streets mostly empty and all the awnings bent against the rain.

"Trouble?" I asked, sitting down.

The queen looked at all of us, and I think decided at that moment that we were no longer little girls. She began to speak to us in a different voice than she usually used, serious and calm.

"There was a riot in Paris yesterday," she said. "Many people were killed. The rioters stormed the old prison, the Bastille." She sighed. "It contained only seven prisoners–four forgers, two madmen, and a duke whose own family had asked that he be imprisoned there. The rioters didn't care about the prisoners. They wanted the ammunition stored in the Bastille."

"Did they get it?" asked Ernestine.

"I imagine so. Not that it matters. We're well protected here. You know the king has soldiers guarding us."

"Then why does it matter?" asked Thérèse.

The queen hesitated. "There were so many people," she said at last. "Like an army–and all fighting. Fighting against–against the government. It's never happened before. And many people died."

"What happens now?" I asked, still thinking of how I had heard no news of this fight in the town. How important could it be?

"I don't know," said the queen.

I wanted to believe that the storming of the Bastille meant nothing, but somehow I could not. In the evening, when I was supposed to be changing into a clean gown before dinner, I rushed across the big courtyard to speak to George. I wanted to know the truth.

I found him in the loft, rolling up his bedding and stuffing his clothing into a bag. "I've joined the National Guard!" he told me. His eyes blazed with excitement. "The militia! Lafayette is the head of it! We're defending Paris!"

"From the king?" I drew my shawl across my shoulders. "Defending Paris from the king?"

"From anything that threatens France." He grabbed my shoulders and kissed me. "Bella–Bella, it's a good thing! I promise. The revolution will make us free–and I'm going to be part of it."

"If you harm the king or queen, you harm me," I said.

"No–" His face grew serious. "Didn't you hear me? The *Marquis de Lafayette* is the head. He wants to protect the king and queen. But he also believes in the rights of the people. It's okay, Bella. It's better than okay–it's wonderful!" He shook my shoulders a little. "Why aren't you happy for me? I'm a soldier now, just like Papa always wanted to be. This is freedom–I got to make a choice."

Nothing bad happened because of the Bastille that I could

see. But three days later, Thérèse and I watched from the Palace windows as the king left for Paris in a carriage. When he returned a few hours later, he seemed to have shrunk. He looked both smaller and older.

He came into the queen's rooms, where we all were, with a cockade in his hat–a little knot of three colors of ribbon, blue, white, and red.

"What's that?" the queen demanded.

The king took off his hat and looked at the cockade. "I'm told it's the new symbol of France," he said. "Red and blue for revolution, white for the king." White–white alone–had always been the king's color. "The mayor of Paris gave it to me on the steps of city hall." He looked at us, his face a mask. "He stood on the step above me," he said, "and he handed it down, and said something about the monarchy and the people united as one."

The queen drew in a sharp breath. Thérèse, Ernestine, and I simply stared. No one, *no one,* stood above the king when they spoke to him. The insolence was beyond imagination.

"Must you wear it?" the queen asked.

The king nodded. "I believe I must." He waddled away, looking less like a king than I'd ever seen.

That night the king's younger brother, the Count of Artois, fled France with all his family. So too did Madame de Polignac. People in Paris hated her because she was a friend of the queen, and she feared she might be killed.

The queen wanted to leave too, but the king refused. "I am the king of France," he said. "What would I be if I left my country?"

"Safe," Thérèse whispered to me in private. "If we left, we would be safe."

Chapter Twenty-four

Now the summer seemed bleak and endless. The king and queen hunted. They rose, they dressed, they ate. They went to Mass and went to bed, the same as ever, always under the eyes of the court–but there were fewer eyes now. Slowly the nobles were fleeing Versailles.

The queen put on a play at the Trianon. We all went to watch it. She acted very lively and happy onstage, as though the horrible summer had not happened, but offstage she still grieved for the Dauphin.

I spent most of the daylight hours at the palace. Maman complained, but I ignored her.

Her joints ached less that summer, for the first time in years. One evening when I returned home I found her making lace. "Maman!" I said.

"Look!" Her fingers were shaking, but they were not very red or swollen, and she could once again hold a needle firmly between them.

"When did that happen?"

"I don't know," she said. "I hardly realized it, but I walk better too." We sat in companionable happiness for a few moments, smiling at each other. "Now that I can make lace again," she said, "I will be able to earn my keep. We will take some of your next quarter-day money and buy your brother a gun."

A gun? For George? "Why does he need one? And why can't he buy his own?"

"They don't pay him to be a guard, you know," Maman said. "And he's not much use in a militia without a gun."

I had heard that the National Guard were all volunteers, but I hadn't believed it. How could so many people live without working? "He ought to get a job," I said. "He has no business being a soldier. He doesn't even know how to fire a gun."

As October began and the weather worsened, the queen stayed among us more and more. She still went to Mass and to her formal meal with the king, but she came to Thérèse's rooms afterward, or called us to hers; the new little Dauphin came to us after his nap. We played with the queen's pug dog and made a few attempts at our embroidery, but some days we simply sat and stared into the fire.

On October fifth the queen spent the morning at the Trianon; she was still there when I arrived at the palace in time to eat dinner with Thérèse. It was raining, a cold, dank, dismal day. By mid-afternoon the queen had come back. She stopped by Thérèse's rooms and asked us to come up to hers. The little Dauphin came too, with his nurse and a handful of toys. "Now we are all snug," the queen said.

At that exact moment a guard came in and announced the arrival of one of the king's ministers. This man rushed through the door looking flustered and agitated. He bowed deeply. The queen stood. "What is it?" she asked.

"Your Majesty, the women of Paris are marching on Versailles."

The queen looked out the window at the steady rain.

"The fishwives, the merchants' wives, the beggars from the streets," the minister continued. His voice trembled, and I noticed that his wig was askew. "Thousands of them, all in a band. All screaming for bread, and for the king to go to Paris, and for the king to accept the assembly's decrees."

The National Assembly spent all their time in Paris making speeches and declaring new laws. The king refused to recognize any of them.

The queen stood still. I couldn't tell what she was thinking. A pack of women did not seem very frightening. On the other hand–thousands? Could there really be thousands?

"Thank you for telling me," the queen said. "The king is hunting. He will return soon."

"Perhaps Your Majesty should leave," the minister said. "Take the children and get away."

She nodded. "When the king returns."

"Pardon me, Your Majesty, but I am not sure you should wait."

The queen nodded and dismissed him. Then she called for the governesses.

Frightened, Thérèse and Ernestine and I began to put away our embroidery. Were we leaving? What would we take? Where would we go? Thérèse's new governess, Madame de Tourzel, sent for some maids to help, and the queen asked the under-governesses to pack our clothing into trunks. "You should each put together a small bag," she told us, "of the things you want to carry inside the carriage."

I went along with Thérèse and Ernestine. A maid gave us

each a tapestry bag. I had nothing to put in mine; I didn't keep anything of my own at the palace, except the ring the queen had given me, which was on my finger, and the box from the king, which was in my pocket. I had been working on an embroidered cushion for the queen. I put that in the bag, and the small pair of silver scissors I used. I saw one of the Dauphin's wooden soldiers behind a chair, and put that in too.

Thérèse kept looking out the windows. Finally I realized that she was looking for the king. When at last he returned from his hunt, we rushed upstairs to the queen's rooms to see him. We assumed we would be leaving at once.

The king could not decide to leave. He consulted with his ministers, and with the queen.

"We can go to Saint-Cloud," the queen said. "Saint-Cloud tonight, and then Austria in the morning."

"A fugitive king?" the king replied. He paced up and down before us. "A *fugitive* king?" He said it as though he found the idea incomprehensible.

"We must leave," the queen insisted. "For the children's sake."

"Should they know that the king their father fled?" he replied.

The conversation went round and round, always covering the same ground. Hours went by and we were still at Versailles. I glanced out the window, anxious. It was growing dark. Shouldn't I return home to my mother? Even while packing the tapestry bag, I'd had a feeling of unreality, as though I were now taking part in a play.

Thérèse saw me look and wrapped her fingers around my wrist. "Stay with me," she said.

"We must go," the queen insisted to the king.

"Would you go without me? You and the children?"

"No, but–"

"But how can I leave? A fugitive king–"

Suddenly we began to hear a far-off noise, like distant thunder or a swarming of bees. The entire afternoon had slipped away while the king dithered. Ernestine went to the window, and drew the curtain aside. "Look," she said. "Here they come."

The women of Paris advanced on the palace like a human flood. They swarmed through the gates and filled the courtyard. They were screaming. As they drew closer, I could see their wide-open mouths and contorted faces. Their noise grew louder and angrier. The women came closer, and closer. There were thousands of them–more and more marching into the courtyard, stretching back on the dim road as far as I could see.

They had been marching for hours in the cold rain. Those at the front, whom I could see clearly, looked like witches, like demons, their wet hair hanging in filthy tangled hanks, their clothes wet and dirty and torn. The smell of them rose up even in the rain, masking the familiar stench of Versailles. They looked beyond anger. They looked evil.

"Come away from the window," said the queen.

We went away and sat on a sofa. There was no question of our leaving now. No carriage could take us through that sea of anger. The Dauphin cried, and his nurse tried to settle him. The queen took him onto her lap, soothing him while darting looks of exasperation at the king. The king sat. Thérèse clenched her hands into fists. Ernestine's eyes were wide and scared. No one seemed to know what to do.

After a time we heard some of the women coming down one of the main halls, not far from where we waited. Palace guards stood at attention near the closed doors to the room. A few moments later one of the ministers came in. "Sire," he said, "they ask that a delegation of women be allowed to speak to you."

The king got up and went out, toward his apartments. We waited in tense silence until he returned. He looked relieved. "They want bread," he said. "That's all. That's all they want from us, and I promised that they should have some."

I slipped away through several adjoining rooms and opened a door to the hallway. The little group of women who had visited the king was just descending toward the foyer. "He has promised bread!" one of them shouted happily.

The crowd responded, not with joy, but with a roar of anger. "A king's promise means nothing!" someone shouted. "The queen will overrule him!" said another. "She'll keep us from our bread!" They began to shout foul, horrible insults about the queen. I crept closer, down the stairwell.

"Bread!" the crowd chanted. "Bread! Bread!"

Some of them looked near starvation. I could see their sunken cheeks, toothless mouths, hollow collarbones. "Bread! Bread!"

Then the chant changed. "We'll cut the queen's throat! We'll use her skin for ribbons!"

Bile rose in my throat. I turned and fled, back to the queen's rooms, slamming the door behind me.

"They want to hurt you," I gasped. "They don't just want bread. And some of them are men." I had seen men standing among the women, armed with pikes and staves.

The king's minister nodded. "Yes," he said. "I saw that too. Even some of the ones dressed as women are, I think, men."

"Why?"

He shrugged, and looked over his shoulder at the king. "To get past the guards, perhaps," he said.

"But why would they want to hurt us?" Thérèse's voice came from the corner, high and plaintive.

Because they are desperate enough to walk twelve miles in a cold rain for the hope of something to eat. Because their children are starving. Because their taxes go to Versailles.

"They don't want to hurt us," the queen said quickly. "They only wished to be heard, and your father has heard them. He will give them bread, and they will go away." She held the Dauphin tight against her. "Nothing will hurt you," she said.

The noise from the courtyard suddenly increased. The minister hurried out. A few moments later he reappeared, looking nervous. "Sire," he said, "the women demand that you put the order for bread into writing." He held out a piece of paper with a trembling hand.

The king stared at it, astonished. "They doubt the king's word?"

The king's word could not be doubted. I knew that.

"Sign it," the queen said. "Sign it quickly. Then they will go away."

The king must have felt the same way. He signed the paper without comment. A few minutes later the noise began to die down, and when we stole a glance out of the windows we saw the tide of women turning, beginning to head back to Paris.

"Where will they get the bread?" I asked.

The queen collapsed in a heap, holding the Dauphin to her. "Oh," she said, "there is grain in the royal storehouses. They can have that, I suppose."

Why hadn't it been given to them already? Why did they have to insist, when they were so obviously in need?

"Well," the king said, with forced heartiness, "the trouble's over." Earlier he had sent for a regiment of soldiers to guard the palace; now he told them to return to their barracks. "We'll have a quiet night." He kissed the queen. "Sleep well, my dear."

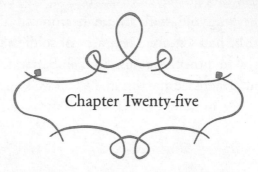

Chapter Twenty-five

"You must stay with us," Thérèse said, clutching my hands.

"But, Thérèse, I–"

"You *must.*" She squeezed my hands so tightly it hurt. I tried to pull away, but she held on. "I forbid you to go," she said. "Besides, it cannot be safe. You'd have to walk through all those women. Who knows what they might do." She paused, and dropped her gaze. "Please. Please stay."

"Oh, all right," I said. I knew Maman would worry, but I also thought Thérèse was right–those women weren't likely to let anyone from the palace pass through their ranks unharmed. If only George would come for me! I ached for Thérèse, for the fear and uncertainty in her eyes, but I ached too for the women wanting bread.

Thérèse, Ernestine, and I retired to Thérèse's bedroom on the ground floor, but we could not sleep and didn't really try. We huddled silently on the bed and watched the embers fall into the fireplace grate. The clock in the room had just chimed midnight when we thought we heard a noise in the hall.

"Only a servant," whispered Ernestine.

"Or one of those women," I said.

"Let's find my mother," said Thérèse.

We hurried through the dark empty passageways. At one point we came to a window where we could look out into the main courtyard. Campfires burned here and there in the royal court, and we could see people moving slowly through the rain.

"They're still here," Ernestine said.

"There's more of them now," Thérèse murmured. "Look how many."

I strained to see through the darkness. Another mob was coming down the street, partially lit by the torches they carried. Mounted soldiers marched at the head of it, with a great white horse in the lead.

I pointed to the horse. Thérèse nodded. Her expression grew so still she looked like a statue.

We watched the soldiers ride through the outer gates. As they approached the inner gates, the king's bodyguards shouted a challenge. We saw the mob stop. In the flickering lights and shadows it was very hard to see anything clearly, but I thought I recognized the rider of the white horse. "The Marquis de Lafayette," I said.

Thérèse exhaled in relief. She grabbed my arm. "Quickly," she said. "He'll go to my father."

We ran on through the back halls. Before long, Thérèse laid her hand flat to a door and carefully opened it a crack. We were looking into the candlelit Oeil-de-Boeuf, the king's receiving room, named for its great window shaped like a bull's-eye. From our narrow vantage point we couldn't see the king or any of his ministers, but a few minutes later, when the Marquis de Lafayette came through a door, we saw him clearly. He was bareheaded, gaunt-eyed, and covered with mud, from his spurred boots to his bald head.

"Sire," said Lafayette, his voice cracking as he gasped for breath. "I come to pledge my allegiance to you."

The king said something in a low voice that we could not hear.

"I ride at the head of the National Guard," Lafayette said, his voice steadier though still ragged with exhaustion. "They insisted–they fear–" He trailed off, then squared his shoulders and began again. "The National Guard has pledged to protect the people of Paris against the Flanders Regiment."

The Flanders Regiment were the hired soldiers protecting the king; the "people of Paris" were that howling mob. So now the National Guard–including my brother, and with Lafayette as its head–was fighting against the king. Fighting against Thérèse's papa. As my brother had promised not to do.

"I have reminded them of their oath to king and country," Lafayette continued. "I have insisted that they reaffirm that oath."

"And yet–," said one of the king's ministers.

"And yet I cannot control them," Lafayette said bitterly. "My choice was to lead them here, or die. They want food, Your Majesty. They want the royal bakeries and storehouses to be opened, and the food distributed to the needy. They want the king and the government moved to Paris."

"As to the first, of course, of course," the king said. "I've already agreed. But Paris–I don't know. Leave Versailles? I don't know." After a pause he said, plaintively, "Can't we wait and decide in the morning?"

"We can't always wait," Lafayette said in a low voice. "Sometimes decisions must be made quickly."

Thérèse let the door softly close. She led us silently through the hallways until we stood near the queen's staircase again. "He won't decide," she said. "He never can decide."

We thought of going to the queen, but now somehow there seemed to be no use. In the end we went wearily back to Thérèse's rooms. We climbed into one bed, our arms around one another, and eventually we fell asleep.

Chapter Twenty-six

A scream ripped through the air, and gunshots, and more screaming. We jumped up, and the maids in our room leapt from their beds on the floor. It was morning; the room was full of light. We could not see anything from Thérèse's windows except the park, so we ran down the long hall past the prince's stairway to a window that overlooked the courtyard. A mob of National Guardsmen had surged through into the inner courtyard. The Black Guard–the king's personal soldiers–tried to hold them back without firing on them. A hail of musketry from the mob brought several guards down.

Now we could hear footsteps running through the halls of the palace, shouts, more screams, then gunfire.

One of the inner doors burst open. It was the queen, half-dressed, with a blanket over her shoulders and her stockings in her hands. "Girls, quick!" she shouted. We followed her through the door into the back passageways and up a hidden stair. "We must get to the king's bedroom," she said. "They are trying to break down the door of mine."

When we reached the door to the king's bedroom, we found it was locked from the other side. The queen pounded on it, calling for the king. No one answered. In panic we turned and ran back along the hall. Somewhere we would find safety.

We met the king, coming down a back stair with the Dauphin in his arms. At his shout a servant opened the door to his room, and then we were all inside it together, all of us, even the king's sister, Madame Elizabeth, and the Princess of Lamballe.

The king was panting, short of breath. "Where is Provence?" he asked, meaning his brother, the Count of Provence.

"Gone," said Madame Elizabeth. "He and his family escaped in the night."

The queen swallowed hard. If she regretted not leaving the day before, she didn't say so. The king merely nodded. I took Thérèse's trembling hand. Outside the room came further screams and shouts. My stomach churned.

Suddenly the door flew open. The Marquis de Lafayette rushed in, his sword drawn and bloody. "Sire!" he said. "Are you safe?"

Through the door I could see one of the palace guards lying dead.

"Oh, what is happening?" cried the queen.

"I will keep you safe," the marquis said. "I pledge it. I swear."

I could not take my eyes off the blood dripping from his sword. Whom had he struck, one of the mob, or one of the guards? Where was my brother, George? I could barely breathe. Beside me Ernestine was crying, and Thérèse looked ready to be sick.

The marquis opened the door to the balcony that overlooked the courtyard and stepped out to face the mob. Howls roared up to greet him. After a few minutes he came back into the room, and asked the king to come out with him.

"The people want to see you," he said.

"Certainly." The king rose and gravely stepped outside. I could hear him speaking to the crowd, but could not make out his words, nor could I understand what they were shouting in return. Whatever it was, I no longer wanted to hear it. I retreated to the far side of the room, and sat on a sofa beside Ernestine. The queen held Louis Charles, and Thérèse clutched the queen's shoulder.

The balcony door opened. "My dear," the king said, "they insist upon seeing you."

Through the open door came catcalls and rude names. Marie Antoinette stood up, gently moving her hand into Thérèse's. She settled the Dauphin more firmly onto her hip. She walked out to the balcony, unsmiling but serene, pulling Thérèse with her. Thérèse's shoulders were trembling, and her face was almost gray. The Dauphin tried to hide his face in his mother's shoulder.

"No, my son," she said to him, gently pulling him upright. "You must be brave. A king of France is always brave."

They stepped out onto that balcony as though they were walking off the face of a cliff.

"No children!" screamed the crowd. "No children!" Someone shouted, "We want the queen!" Another cried, "The queen's head! Her head on a platter!"

The Dauphin and Thérèse came back into the room. They collapsed together on a sofa near the balcony door. Ernestine and I ran to them. Thérèse was shaking from head to foot, and the Dauphin was sobbing.

"Those monsters!" Thérèse said. "They are *monsters*!"

"They are hungry," I whispered. "All they want is bread."

Thérèse looked up at me, amazed. "How can you say that?"

she asked. "They are killing the palace guards! They threaten my mother! And you speak up for them?"

"If you had not made me your lacemaker, I might have been starving too," I said. "And my mother. We would not have been able to earn enough to eat."

"So you would have marched against me?" Thérèse asked bitterly. She drew her little brother to her and rocked him back and forth. "You would have threatened my mother the queen?"

"No," I said. I knelt beside her and forced her to take my hand. "Look at me, Thérèse. I never would have. I never could have, because I know you. I love you, and I know that you love me. We are true friends. But if I had never met you–if my own mother were starving–"

Thérèse took a deep breath and rocked back and forth. "Yes," she murmured at last. "Yes, I do see. I didn't know–I didn't know there were people like that."

Ernestine said quietly, "There are so many."

Thérèse's fingers tightened around mine. "But you are my true friend. Whatever happens, you cannot desert me. You must stay with me. I need you."

From the balcony, the catcalls turned to cheers. "Long live General Lafayette! Long live the queen!" I did not know what Lafayette had done, but somehow he'd diverted the crowd once again.

They came back into the room, the king looking badly shaken, but the queen remaining calm. "You have saved us," she said to Lafayette. "Now, can you save the poor palace guards? They are being slaughtered."

"Bring me one," he told her. "The younger the better."

One of the ministers rushed downstairs and came back with

a guard. I knew that noblemen's sons could join the palace guard as young as fourteen years old, but this guard looked even younger–he was nothing but a frightened boy. Tears streaked his smooth cheeks.

"Come out on the balcony," Lafayette said. "Don't be afraid." He led the boy out. We watched through the open door as Lafayette removed the boy's white cockade–part of his uniform, the symbol of the king–and dropped it over the balcony's edge. Then Lafayette removed the tricolor cockade from his own hat, pinned it onto the boy's hat, and embraced him.

A great cheer went up from the crowd. "Long live the revolution! Long live France!"

Lafayette escorted the boy back inside. "Tell all the guards to put on the tricolor," he said. Then he looked at the king. "You must go to Paris," he said wearily. "Sire, you must."

If the king noticed that now even the Marquis de Lafayette was commanding him, he gave no sign. "Order the carriages," he said. "Order anything you like. We will go at once."

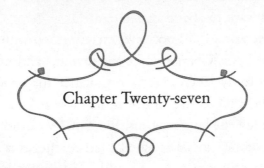

Chapter Twenty-seven

The Marquis arranged for a carriage. He went out and spoke to the crowd, assuring them that they could escort the king to Paris. Inside, the maids flew about, packing the things the royal family would take with them. The king's ministers made hurried lists of papers to bring.

"Where will we go?" the queen asked.

"Paris," said the king, as though it were a specific place, a house where they would live. The truth, I guessed, was that nobody knew.

I should leave now, I thought. This was the catastrophe George had warned me about. I would go home to Maman, and be a lacemaker again. The fear the royal family felt was almost tangible; it gnawed at me, but I was not part of it.

"I'm going," I said to Thérèse.

She clutched at me and at Ernestine. "You can't!" she said. Her fingers tore the sleeve of my nightgown. "You can't leave me!"

The queen paused in her preparations. "You and Ernestine of course will come," she said. "You are part of our family too."

I didn't want to be part of Thérèse's family. I didn't want to be one of her ladies, and dress up, and dance, and close my eyes to the truth. I didn't want to pretend anymore.

Nor did I want to abandon Thérèse.

In my indecision I did nothing, merely stood with Ernestine, Thérèse, and Louis-Charles while the servants and the king and queen made ready. Thérèse took my silence for agreement; she smiled wanly and held on to my arm.

When we left the king's rooms, the hallway outside them was slippery. A strange metallic smell masked the usual stench of the palace–I could not place it, until I put it together with the half-dried red puddles on the floor.

Blood. The hallways were covered with blood. I caught my breath in one great gasp and tried to lift my skirts away from it, and as I did I turned a little sideways and saw one of the guards lying on the floor, dead, his sightless eyes staring straight ahead. A young guard. No older than George.

George, I thought. *Oh, George, please save me.* He always had. I turned my head this way and that, looking for him. *George.*

"Don't look," Ernestine said, elbowing me from behind. "It's better if we don't look."

Slowly, carefully, guarded and led by the Marquis's drawn sword, we made our way to the door. The great crowds in the courtyards were growing agitated again. Hordes of people tried to force their way into the palace. Palace guards and National Guardsmen–working together now, and all wearing the revolutionary cockade–held them off. The Marquis thrust his way forward, and then we were outside. The crowd cheered. The king looked as though he didn't know what to do, but the queen bowed to them, and they cheered again. The carriage waited by the door. The servants were tying trunks to it. The

Marquis swung himself onto his white horse, which someone had brought forward for him. In another moment we would be away.

I felt a hand on my arm–a soft hand, a gentle one. "George!" I said, whirling around.

It was Maman. Maman, who said she would never go to the palace again. Maman, who had fought her way through that terrible crowd.

"Isabella," she said quietly, "it's time to come home."

Now my own knees began to shake; the terror I'd kept at bay engulfed me. "Oh, Maman," I said. "How can I–"

Thérèse turned, and saw my mother standing beside me. Her eyes filled with tears. She put her hand on my arm, but this time, instead of clutching me, she pushed me away. "You have always been my true friend," she said. "Get away from here while you still can."

The queen stepped into the carriage, carrying the Dauphin. Ernestine stepped in next. "Ernestine!" I called. "Wait! Come with Maman and me." To Thérèse I said, "I would take you, too, if I could." Not that the crowd would have let the king's daughter escape. Thérèse gave no sign that she'd heard me. She climbed into the carriage without looking back. "Send Ernestine out!" I called, trying to reach the carriage door. "Ernestine!" The door shut; the horses started. The carriage rolled slowly forward. A great cheer went up from the mob.

People surrounded the carriage on all sides as it trundled slowly toward the road. In a matter of minutes, the courtyard had begun to empty. I looked at Maman, who was supporting herself with her walking stick. "Can you walk home?" I asked.

"I have never felt stronger," Maman replied.

I took her arm to steady her, just in case. Carefully we made our way past the carnage in the courtyard, away from the palace, down the streets toward home.

All day long carriages and wagons pulled away from the palace in a steady unending stream. Servants left with the king's possessions; courtiers left with everything they could carry. The town of Versailles emptied too. All around us, wig makers and mantua makers and tailors took down their awnings and packed up their stores.

By the time Maman reached our apartment, she was tired. I made a pot of tea and took a cup to her while she rested in bed. Then I went to the window. I hated to look out, to see the entire world I had known fall to pieces. Instead I picked up the length of lace I was working on from the shelf beneath the window. I threaded a needle and began to cover one of the ground lines with tiny, even knots. My fingers flew. I was as good a lacemaker as my mother, and my grandmother before her. It was a good thing. We would need my talents now.

"Oh, Isabelle," my mother called out in a tired voice. "Put away that needle. Don't you understand? No one in France will buy lace now."

Chapter Twenty-eight

Maman was right. Overnight, lace became a symbol of the hated aristocracy. Revolutionaries dressed plainly. Nobles, and all they had done, and everything they had stood for, were despised. Worse, they were threatened. Some of them were killed.

Maman and I stayed in our rooms for over a month. We went out only to get bread from the baker, or wood for our fire. We traded some of our household goods for food. Maman had a small pile of coins saved, but refused to part with any of them. "Who knows what we shall need?" she said. She traded our mirror, some of our dishes, Grand-mère's old clothes. "The more we get rid of now, the easier it will be when we move."

"Where are we going?" I asked.

Maman shrugged. "Wherever George takes us, I suppose."

The town grew quieter and quieter. Even Maman and I barely spoke to each other. We lived in a perpetual haze. Worry made us tired, and yet also made it impossible to sleep.

We expected George daily, but he never came.

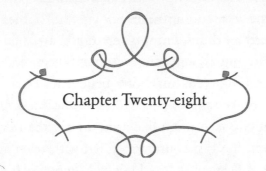

One crisp day in mid-November, I suggested we go to the palace. I wanted to see it one more time. I knew, from talking to the baker in town, that the royal family was being held at the king's old palace in Paris, called the Tuileries. I knew nothing more. I hoped the Tuileries was like Versailles, hoped Thérèse and Ernestine were riding their ponies–the stables had been emptied, though I didn't know where the horses had gone–and the little Dauphin was playing with his hoops in some wide green parkland. I hoped, but didn't believe it.

The gates of Versailles had been shut and locked. The huge stone building looked more like a mountain than ever, a desolate mountain, the vast courtyards filled with trash and piles of autumn leaves. I knew that if I walked far enough around the palisade, I would find a gate I could open, and I was sure that when I got inside the gates I could find a way into the palace itself, but suddenly I no longer wanted to. "Better to remember it happy," Maman whispered. I nodded.

We walked across the street to the beautiful empty stables. I wanted to go inside, but feared being hit with memories of George with his pitchfork, his thin face smiling, talking while he worked. I looked up at the enormous building.

Then I saw, on the corner of the street, a face I recognized. Pierre. Pierre the candle boy.

"Isabelle!" he cried when he saw me.

I waved him over. "We are looking for my brother," I said. "My brother, George, he worked in the stables."

Pierre touched his hat, where the revolutionary cockade fluttered. "I'm sorry, sister," he said.

Maman gasped. I grabbed Pierre's arm. "You know him? Where is he? What happened?"

"He was a guardsman, like me," Pierre said. I nodded. Pierre crossed himself. "He died valiantly. I'm sorry to tell you. But he died fighting for a good cause."

Grief hit me like a battering ram. "A good cause?" I shouted. "A *good cause*! What cause is good enough for that?"

"Liberty," Pierre said. "Equality. Fraternity. He fought for what he believed in. I know. I fought at his side."

Maman was weeping, keening, a noise horrible to hear.

"Fighting the king," I said. "Fighting against the king."

Pierre kept his hand on my arm. I tried to shake him off. "Listen," he said. "He died defending the Marquis. The morning the palace was being overrun? The guards slaughtered? That mob planned to kill the king."

"I was there," I said flatly. "I was with the king."

"Then you know too that they tried to kill the Marquis," Pierre said, "because he prevented them from killing the king. A man nearly ran the Marquis through with a pikestaff–but your brother got in the way."

So they'd killed George instead. And we hadn't known it. While Maman and I had walked home from Versailles, George had lain somewhere in that vast courtyard, dead. And he was buried in an unmarked grave without a Mass being sung.

"I'm sorry," Pierre said again. "I was part of the group that escorted the king to Paris. I didn't know George had fallen. Another guard told me about it later. This is the first I've been able to leave Paris. I would have tried to come earlier–" He swallowed. "I didn't realize you didn't know."

Maman's sobs continued as though Pierre were not there.

"We grew to be friends," Pierre said. "Your brother and me. We both were proud to be in the guard."

"Stupid pride," I said. Yet the thought came to me that George had indeed saved me one last time. If the mob had killed the

Marquis, they would have killed the king, too, and perhaps all of us who were with him.

I would have taken my chances, I thought. I would have rather faced the mob empty-handed than lost George.

Pierre followed us home. I wasn't sure why. I put Maman to bed and drew our two chairs up to the fire. I poured cider, and set out a loaf of bread. "What will you do?" Pierre asked. He ate, but I wasn't hungry.

I shrugged. "What is there to do? I suppose we will go to Paris. There must be work there, yes?"

"I'm not sure," Pierre said.

"I'm good with a needle. Even if it's not lacemaking, I'll find something." I was glad Pierre was there but at the same time wished he'd go away. I didn't want to cry for George until I was alone.

"I'll take you to Paris, if you like. Perhaps we can find a cart for your things."

I nodded glumly. "You'll escort us," I said to Pierre, "the way you escorted the king."

Chapter Twenty-nine

Maman and I went to Paris and the revolution descended into madness. In the beginning I kept waiting for Lafayette to take over–I hadn't forgotten how he'd served both sides that night at the palace, protecting the royal family and placating the revolutionaries–but he never did. I don't know why. Instead we had a succession of men to whom revolution meant blood; every time someone different took over, another wave of people died. A new invention called a "guillotine" chopped off heads with a blade on a pulley. It was supposed to be kinder than using an ax.

"Dead is dead," Maman said, and I agreed.

After a few weeks of searching, and after we'd come right to the end of our money, Maman and I managed to find work at a tavern in Paris. Maman cooked and served at the bar; I washed dishes and mugs and tables and the floor. We earned almost no pay, but we got our meals and could sleep by the kitchen fire on the floor. It was a far cry from the comfort of our own apartment, much less Thérèse's rooms. But I tried very hard not to think of Thérèse. It would be dangerous to speak of her; our tavern was packed every night with revolutionaries cursing the king. Riots were common in Paris, and the streets were dangerous; in the tavern we were both safe and fed. The tavern owner, though taciturn, was kind, Maman's joints were tolerable, and we knew we were lucky compared to most.

I could not help wondering what use it all was. How was anyone benefiting by this? What good had this turmoil done?

Pierre tried to explain it to me. For the first few months he stopped by the tavern every week or so to see how we were. "Don't you see?" he said. "The common people have a voice now. The church and nobles will pay taxes, the burden of the government will be shared, and the common people will be able to buy food."

"I could buy food before," I said. Except that I couldn't have, without Thérèse's help.

"You were never common," Pierre said, reminding me of this without mentioning Thérèse's name.

I waved my hand. George was dead, and I didn't care about revolution.

One evening Pierre stayed at the tavern late, until Maman had banked the fire and I was wiping the last of the tables down. A few old drunkards dozed in one corner, but soon the tavern owner would kick them out and bar the door.

"I saw your friend, that princess," he said when I picked up his mug to wipe under it.

"You did?" My hand froze on the tabletop, and I checked over my shoulder to be sure the tavern owner hadn't heard. Maman and I never even admitted we'd come from the town of Versailles. "Where was she? Did she look well?"

"She was walking in the gardens at the Tuileries. She looked well enough. Hardly pretty, is she?"

I ignored that. "Was Ernestine with her? The Dauphin?"

"She seemed alone to me."

I gathered an armful of empty mugs and took them to be washed. When I went past him again, he said, "I could take you there, if you like."

"I don't know," I said. "I–"

"Time's up," the tavern owner called. He hoisted one of the drunkards up and hauled him out the door.

"Think about it," Pierre said. "We'll talk when I return."

Pierre never returned. Maman and I never saw him again. Nor could we find out what had happened to him. He might have gotten sick; he might have been killed in a riot or an accident. He might have simply left Paris, though I couldn't believe he wouldn't have let me know.

I wasn't sure I liked France anymore.

Thérèse had always said that the emperor of Austria would come to the queen's aid, but he didn't. If he or any of the other rulers of Europe were upset that the French king was imprisoned in his own palace, they never said. They waited. The king waited. I waited. I worked from morning until late at night, every day but Sundays. I outgrew my only dress, and hadn't money to buy another. My hands were permanently chapped from dishwater. Maman's back hurt from bending over the fire.

"What are we doing here?" I asked Maman one day.

"You've got a better idea?" she said.

Some days I did have a better idea. I began to form a plan, but I couldn't bring myself to tell Maman. I thought of Thérèse, and I prayed for her safety, and I knew that while she still waited for the revolution to end, I would too.

Two years went by.

Then one afternoon there was excitement in the tavern. "They've escaped, the Capets! Flown the coop!" The Capets were what the revolutionaries called the royal family. I grew very interested in sweeping the tavern floor while I listened.

They'd slipped out of the Tuileries one by one, late at night, disguised: the king, the queen, Louis Charles, and Thérèse. They'd left Paris in a traveling coach.

I remembered the day at Versailles when the queen had urged the king to flee. "A fugitive king?" he'd said, as though he could not believe such a thing were possible. "A fugitive king?"

"He finally made up his mind," I told Maman.

The next day we heard they'd been caught. It was remarkable how quickly the news traveled. They'd almost made it to the Austrian border, where they would have been safe, before the National Guard soldiers caught up with them. The trip took them twice as long as it should have because the coach the king had wanted was large and slow, and because he'd stopped several times to eat during the journey.

Two days later I put down my dishcloth and joined the crowd of Parisians that had gathered to see them return. They came up the road toward the Tuileries slowly, the huge carriage surrounded by National Guardsmen. People stood three and four deep on both sides of the road, watching silently. No one jeered or called out. I shoved my way forward.

The coach was covered with dust. Through its open windows everyone could see the king and queen, sitting very upright and still. I craned forward. The Dauphin sat on someone's knee across from the king. *Look out the window, Thérèse,* I silently willed her. *Look.*

She didn't. I thought I caught a glimpse of her shoulder, but I couldn't be sure.

The royals were put into a prison, not a palace. It was called the Temple.

When I heard that, I went to Maman. "This is the end," I said. "The king will never escape now. I think we should leave."

For two years people had been leaving France, nobles and craftspeople, anyone whose livelihood depended on the Old Regime.

"Oh, yes, let's," Maman said.

"America would be best, but it's harder to get to than England," I said, "so England might be better. I hear a lot of French people live in England now."

"Oh, as to that, who can say?" Maman said. "Since money is no object, why not go farther? I hear China is a fine and temperate place." Her eyes crinkled. "It's good to hear you joking at last."

"Maman, I'm not joking! I want to get away."

She sobered. "Yes, of course. So do I. So does half of Paris. But we can't even afford cloth to cover you decently. Isabelle, if we had the money to leave, we would have left long ago."

I wouldn't have left. I had been waiting, to see what would happen to Thérèse. Now I looked over Maman's shoulder at the empty taproom. I pulled her farther into the kitchen. I reached deep into my pocket and pulled out a wad of rags. I unwound the rags and unwrapped the king's little box. From under the torn lining of my shoe I took the box's key. I unlocked the box, and opened it.

"Oh," said Maman. She held up the queen's little diamond ring. It sparkled in the light. Maman turned it round in her hand. Very quickly she put the ring back, closed the box, and pushed it into my hands. "I thought you'd left that at the palace," she said. "I never knew you were so clever, Isabelle. All this time to never say a word."

"Will it bring enough?" I asked.

"For passage to England, yes. Not America. But it would get us to England, I think, if we are clever and careful and sharp."

"We are clever and careful," I said.

She nodded. "So we are."

All the rest of the day while we worked, Maman and I exchanged secret smiles. I flexed my roughened, work-reddened hands. Soon enough I would be in a new country. My hands would heal, and I would be a lacemaker again.

Author's Note

This book is fiction; Isabelle, her family, and her association with the court of Louis XVI are entirely made up.

However, my story would have been possible. Marie Antoinette was fond of children, and there are several instances recorded of her paying special attention to a particular child–rescuing a small boy from being run over by a coach, then taking him back to the Palace to be cleaned and fed; allowing one of her maid's children to stay in her rooms at Versailles; talking to children she encountered on her travels.

Ernestine was a real historical figure. The daughter of a chambermaid and a bailiff, she was brought up to be the companion of the queen's eldest daughter, Marie-Thérèse (called Thérèse). Her real name was Marie-Philippine Lambriquet, but she was indeed called Ernestine because the queen thought it was more fashionable. She was dressed the same as Thérèse, and was taught alongside her. Her expenses are listed in the government accounts of the Children of France–the children of the king and queen. Following Ernestine's mother's death in 1788, Ernestine became a permanent resident of Versailles (even though her father and grandparents were still alive). She was taken to the Tuileries, and rescued by her grandparents sometime before 1792. Some accounts have her accompanying the royal family on their escape attempt, but most do not. She died in 1814.

When the royal family failed in their escape attempt, the tenor of the revolution began to change. All along there had been people who no longer wanted France to have a king, not even a king who didn't rule. In 1792 the National Assembly abolished the monarchy. Yet it was difficult to imagine the king becoming a regular citizen–and he himself had no intention of becoming one. The royal family was taken from the Tuileries and put under arrest in the Temple prison. Anyone who spoke in their favor, or attempted to help them, was put to death.

Louis XVI was never a strong leader. There were times when he could have compromised with the revolutionary leaders, and very probably saved himself, but he could not imagine himself as anything but the absolute ruler of France. He wanted to be restored to his full powers, and he secretly lobbied the heads of other nations–particularly Austria, which his wife's brother ruled–to help him defeat the revolution.

Several months after the royal family's attempted escape, Austria declared war on France. The revolutionaries immediately condemned the king to death for treason. Louis XVI was guillotined on January 21, 1793.

Leaders of other European nations were horrified, and many countries declared war on France. Lafayette had been banished from Paris in early 1792. The main leader of the rebellion, Robespierre, tried to remain in control by seizing and executing all who opposed him. This time became known as the Reign of Terror. Hundreds of people went to the guillotine. Many more fled France. Among those killed included the Princess of Lamballe, Madame Elizabeth, and the queen herself, on October 16, 1793. She was executed after a brief trial in which she defended herself so well against false accusations that the crowd, primed to hate her, believed her instead.

The little Dauphin, Louis Charles, was taken away from his

mother and sister several weeks before the queen's death. The queen could hear his sobs through the prison's walls. He was locked in a small cell and left alone without warmth or companionship; he was barely fed. He probably had tuberculosis as well. His uncle, the Count of Provence, who was safely in exile, officially declared him King Louis XVII, but the little boy never knew it. He died on or near June 8, 1795, after years of misery.

Since women did not rule in France, Thérèse was not considered the threat to the revolution that the rest of her family was. She continued to live in the Temple for a time.

When Robespierre died, the Reign of Terror came to an end. Thérèse was allowed to go to her uncles in exile and married one of her cousins, the Duke of Angoulême. She had no children. She died in 1851.